FINAL THOUGHTS . . .

"Good evening."

The voice, almost in his ear, hit him like a thunderclap. For a bare moment he was unable to move. He had never been so startled in his life.

His mind was racing. A cop, it had to be a cop. Consenting adults, that's what they were, and fornication wasn't an offense anymore. Embarrassing, hell for the girl, but she'd live through it. After all, she'd been had a good many times before.

Then he felt a cold piece of cold metal press against his forehead, and terror flooded him until he couldn't even jibber.

"Don't move," the voice commanded. "Stay exactly the way that you are."

He couldn't have moved for anything. It was all that he could do to keep breathing. Only his mind worked, and because he was used to tight corners, he managed to speak. "My wallet's on the front seat. Help yourself. I'm insured." He started to rise.

"I said, don't move."

He froze in compliance, despite the total awkwardness of his position.

The hard steel was still against his head. "Now, Mr. San Marco, you've come to the end of the road. You have just screwed somebody for the last time."

"*No!*" he shrieked. The sound was still in his throat when the first silenced bullet hit him.

He never felt the second. . . .

A KILLING
IN THE MARKET

by John Ball

MEDALLION BOOKS LOS ANGELES

A KILLING IN THE MARKET

A Medallion Books edition. Originally published by
Doubleday & Company, Inc., as
The Killing in the Market.

First printing, July 1986

Second printing, August 1986

ISBN: 1-55627-002-X

Art direction by Alyson Dunn

Cover illustration by David Mann

The Medallion name and Medallion logotype
are trademarks of Medallion Books, Inc.

MEDALLION BOOKS, INC.
5455 Wilshire Boulevard, Suite 1700
Los Angeles, California 90036

Printed in the United States of America

For
Christianna Brand
with admiration and love

1

Two hundred feet after the lead car of the long commuter train had bitten into the half-mile curve that ended at Boylesport station, the engineer began to feed compressed air through the triple valves precisely as he had done hundreds of times before. In response the steel brake shoes clamped against the spinning wheels, and the screech of metal against metal shuddered through the air. The train had already dropped a good half of its original passenger load, and the long coaches were no longer filled with the fetid air of New York City. Once again there was the illusion that Manhattan and all that it contained had been left forgettably far behind.

The station and its platform had been designed to perform a standard public function, so it was very like most of the other stations on the line with nothing about it to show that it had been selected to serve a privileged community. It ignored the fact that Boylesport had become synonymous with wealth; the real estate prices were astronomical, even for one of the most fashionable parts of the Long Island south shore. Boylesport was made up principally of

estates, some paid for and some not, but all of them
in varying degrees impressive.

The moment that the train braked to a stop, passengers began to disembark. A few were in a visible
hurry, some were merely brisk. Most of the rest
were carefully casual. Mr. Nathan Lockheim took
his time so that he would not have to endure jostling
or any other such indignities.

Along the station platform there was a long row of
parked cars, waiting as they did each business day
for their owners to return from the city and drive
them home. As Mr. Lockheim walked with dignity
past them, he noted as he did each time that the
majority of them were compacts and small foreign
cars. Some Volvos were in evidence, and an occasional Mercedes, but for the most part they were in
the seven- to eight-thousand-dollar bracket. The
knowledge of this fact gave Mr. Lockheim a certain
sense of inner warmth. They were something like
troops with himself the reviewing general.

Mr. Lockheim's car was a Cadillac El Dorado
which gleamed with custom gold paint. He unlocked
it with a sense of appropriate fitness; the ordinari-
ness of the train he could not help, but now he was
not about to be seen driving a Toyota.

Comfortably settled behind the wheel, he started
the engine and listened to its contented purr. Satisfied, he adjusted the air conditioning and then
turned on the stereo tape player. Immediately he
was surrounded by soothing sounds of his own
choosing as he pressed the automatic door lock that

insured his privacy. When he was fully ready he backed out, cutting off a new Granada whose driver had to jump on the brake to avoid a collision, shifted the automatic transmission lever to *drive*, and rolled in comfort off the parking lot.

Mr. Lockheim was in a very good mood. His hard week's work had resulted in a handsome profit, one he had realized barely ten minutes before the market had closed. He had been ten thousand short on Sphinx Wire and Cable, a position it had taken him four days to acquire without tipping his hand. The stock had been up on the expectation of the passage of the Alaska Communications Complex bill, something that the military had been pushing for with all of its muscle. When the bill had failed, due to some unexpected vote switches on the floor of the House, SXC had hit the skids for five and one-eighth points. After he had covered his short positions, he had cleared an average profit of four and seven eighths per share. That was very close to fifty thousand dollars, and there were many many weeks during the year when he did not do as well as that.

He passed through the center of the small community at a dignified pace. He felt assured that the Boylesport Police would know better than to stop his car, but he drove carefully anyway since he was not a man compelled to hurry. His dignity was precious to him, and he took pains to protect it. At the intersection where he always turned left he signaled and then made the corner just ahead of a housewife at the wheel of her Chevrolet station wagon, who had been coming the other way. When the Chevrolet swung in behind him, Mr. Lockheim pressed the accelerator and spurted away. The music kept him relaxed and contented.

Eight minutes later he slowed before the entrance drive to his own splendid estate. It was a small ceremony to him—the moment that the public highway was behind him, he would become, quite literally, master of all he surveyed. Since two cars were coming toward him, he elected to use the turn signal. It was proper, of course, and it also served to point out to those who might be interested where it was that he lived. He raised his right hand and flipped the lever down.

Instantly he was stunned by a sheet of flame that seemed to surround him. A frightful shock of sound slammed against his eardrums as the seat erupted under him. He was conscious that he was being thrown through the air as the impact of unbearable pain smote him like a hammer. He landed hard with the windshield frame on top of him; searing heat tore at his legs.

He gasped for air and had to fight to get it into his lungs. A violent sense of outrage filled him; his mind refused all other thoughts. As the pain mounted he wanted desperately to fight back, but his body ignored his commands. Then someone had him by the shoulders and was dragging him across the road, away from his flaming car. He heard someone say, "It's all right. I called for help on my CB radio. Just take it easy now."

He wanted to scream in protest, but the voice in his throat would not come out. He began to see only a dim redness. He tried to raise himself up to issue a command, but failed. The last thing that he heard was an approaching siren as he lay in his agony at the edge of the public highway.

The first patrol car to respond was driven by Officer Frank Happs who was twenty-seven and who had been a sworn member of the force for a little less than two years. Without getting out of his car he took a quick look and then radioed in for all of the backup that was available. The ambulance was already on the way; as he pulled to one side he could see it coming down the road.

As soon as Happs's call came in Lieutenant John Harbizon knew without being told that whatever had happened, it was his baby. Not very much of a violent nature occurred in the well-settled community, but when anything did Harbizon was the acknowledged specialist. He had been through the FBI school and he was the automatic delegate to most of the law enforcement seminars to which the Boylesport Police was invited.

Harbizon responded in one of the three unmarked cars that the department had available. Because the community was small, they were useless for any sort of undercover work, but occasionally calls had to be made at some of the status-conscious estates where a conspicuously marked police car might not be welcome. It took him a little more than five minutes to reach the scene; as he got out in front of the Lock-heim estate he was very much aware that he was confronted with the first car bombing he had ever been called upon to handle.

Happs had his patrol unit properly positioned with the roof lights on, keeping traffic away from the grisly scene. A second unit, on the other side of the wreck, was doing the same thing. The ambulance men were standing by; they had covered the body with a blanket. At the gateway to the estate a little Latin-appearing maid was staring with huge, frightened eyes.

Harbizon lost no time whatever. He went first to the maid and spoke to her briefly, keeping his voice calm as he did so. "Please go back inside," he told her. "You can see that there's been an accident. We'll come in to see you shortly."

The little maid looked at him for a few stricken seconds, then she turned and almost fled back up the private driveway. Harbizon did not wait to watch her; as soon as he saw her start back he was inter-cepted by one of the ambulance men. "The victim is a Nathan Lockheim," he said. "He's dead, no doubt about it whatever. The man who pulled him away from his car is here if you want to talk to him."

"I do," Harbizon snapped. "And I need a doctor to pronounce the man dead."

"He's on his way."

"Good." He turned to Happs who was standing by. "Call in and ask to have a road block set up at each end of this stretch. Emergency vehicles and residents only to be allowed through."

"Got it," Happs said, and moved to obey.

The fire department had a single pumper on hand. The engineer in charge of it told him, "We foamed the fire and then left everything as it was. We have a damn good arson man available if you want him."

"Ask him to come, by all means," Harbizon answered. He knew perfectly well that the arson man was good, but that was not the time to say so. "Stand by if you can. We'll want a washdown after the body has been removed."

The fire department engineer nodded and returned to his vehicle. As he did so, Harbizon walked rapidly to where the citizen who had pulled Lockheim away from his flaming car was patiently waiting, watching everything that was going on. "Tell me what happened," Harbizon invited.

The would-be rescuer was concise and accurate. He told how he had seen the big gold Cadillac slowing up, apparently to turn into the driveway. The turn signal had blinked once just as the car had exploded. The driver had not had his seat belt fastened, but it would have made little difference. He wasn't sure exactly how the man had come out of the car, but he had the impression that he had come through the windshield. He did remember that the windshield frame had been lying across the victim's body. He surmised that it had been a pop out type that would let go in the event of enough force from the inside. He had seized the victim by the shoulders and had pulled him backward, face up, to the side of the road. He had given a very quick call on his CB radio, but he wasn't sure that it had been effective. He had returned to his car and had put out a broadcast asking for police and emergency medical help.

Harbizon took his card and thanked him warmly for his timely and responsible action. Clearly the man was not afraid to get involved, and in the greater New York area, that was a novelty. Undoubtedly he would turn out to be a member of some volunteer group such as the Civil Air Patrol; it would fit the pattern.

Harbizon went back to his car and took out some of the camera equipment he carried in the trunk. With a Rolleiflex he made a series of six shots of the car wreckage, planning them so that every angle was carefully covered. He had the cover removed from the body and took six more shots, following the same procedure. The exact position of the body would mean little, but he saw superficially that the way it lay fully backed up the story the rescuer had told him.

While he was working an intern arrived, bent briefly over the corpse, and then formally pronounced it dead. Harbizon nodded to the ambulance men that it could be taken away. The mess had to be cleaned up and the road reopened to normal traffic as soon as possible. At the fringes of the operation three wreckers were waiting, red lights blinking, each hoping for the bonanza of what would be an expensive job. One of the drivers even tried to begin operations before Harbizon abruptly waved him away. There was a police wrecker that was shared with two other nearby communities, and the men riding it would know how to take care of evidence.

He wanted to explore the still warm wreck, but his judgment dictated that it would be best to let the fire department arson expert do that. Instead he bent over the body just before it was to be moved and extracted the wallet from the inner coat pocket. He flipped it open and examined some of the credit cards that it contained. He also checked the address. In Boylesport almost everyone was a person of some importance, and influence surrounded it like a corona. Harbizon's thoroughness was his chief asset in addition to his professional training. In order to do his sworn duty in such an environment, he had to be sure of every step that he took. He had learned that hard lesson many years ago.

By that time there were five officers on the scene, the road blocks were up, and things were working properly. The next job was to see the people in the house. Once more he turned to Happs, whose ashen look had gradually disappeared. "I'm going inside," he said. "Care to come along?"

Happs had sense enough not to ask if it would be all right to leave his unit; the answer was obvious. Aware that the scene ahead of him might be a rough one, he fell in beside the lieutenant and walked up the driveway toward the house.

When they were still twenty feet short of the door it was opened by the same little maid. A butler stood waiting inside. A butler! Harbizon knew that there were a few in Boylesport and that most of them were there to support the never-ending game of social upmanship that seemed to amuse the very rich, or those who just missed being in that category.

As the butler stepped forward, Harbizon held out his badge in its case. "I'm Lieutenant Harbizon," he said simply.

"My name is Harkness, lieutenant."

"Thank you. You're aware, of course, that there's been a terrible accident outside."

"Yes, sir, we know."

"I don't want to put this too abruptly," Harbizon said, "but are you also aware that there was a fatality?"

"Yes, lieutenant, we understand that Mr. Lockheim was killed. Is that correct?"

"I'm afraid that it is."

For just a moment the butler hesitated, then he asked, "How did he die, sir?"

"It appears as though a bomb of some kind may have been attached to his car. You understand that that hasn't been established as yet."

"Yes, lieutenant, I understand perfectly. How may I help you?"

Harbizon couldn't help liking him. The man was obviously intelligent, and he handled himself well. Of course, there was no indication yet as to how well he had gotten along with his employer. Presumably well enough, because Nathan Lockheim had been known as a man who liked to have things very much his own way. If the butler had not given complete satisfaction, no sentimental considerations would have interfered with his replacement.

"If I could speak with Mrs. Lockheim, it might be most helpful. I realize, of course, that she has sustained a very severe shock."

Harkness kept all expression off his face. "Madam is indeed terribly shocked, but fortunately she has"—the butler sought for words—"great strength of character."

Harbizon caught the inference clearly, and while Happs waited patiently in the background, he explored it. "Mr. Harkness, you understand that Mr. Lockheim's death is definitely a police matter."

"I am aware, sir, that it was not an accident."

"Precisely. So before I speak with Mrs. Lockheim, if she can see me, I want to ask you a question or two in complete confidence." He turned toward his patrolman. "You understand that, Happs?"

"Yes, sir. Not a word to anyone."

Harbizon chalked one up for his subordinate; that had been exactly the right answer.

"What do you want to know, sir?" Harkness asked.

Harbizon checked that the maid was gone. "Has anyone perhaps been trying to win Mrs. Lockheim's affections?"

The butler held his face immobile, but his voice was definite. "I very much doubt that, sir."

"Do you know of any possible interest Mr. Lockheim may have taken in, quite frankly, a married woman?"

There was a microscopic pause before that question was answered. "I know of no one offhand, lieutenant, who would fit that description. That is, a married woman in whom Mr. Lockheim was interested."

Those questions had been the warm up. Harbizon put the key one in the same tone of voice, almost as if it were an afterthought. "The relationship between Mr. and Mrs. Lockheim—I would appreciate your comment on that."

"Sir, you understand my position . . ."

"Absolutely, Mr. Harkness, and your confidence will not be violated. If I know now, I may be able to avoid more public exposure later on."

"In view of that statement, lieutenant, I might say that Mr. and Mrs. Lockheim maintained diplomatic relations. I do not believe that they lavished a great deal of affection on each other."

"Thank you. Will you see now if Mrs. Lockheim can see us?" He almost said "receive," but caught himself in time.

At that moment the little maid appeared again, apparently to see if she were wanted. "Gretchen," the butler said to her, "please inquire if madam can receive two gentlemen from the police."

As soon as the girl had gone, Harbizon put a one word question. "Gretchen?"

"Her name, sir, is actually Maria, but madam desires her to answer to Gretchen, so she does so."

Harbizon did not comment as he followed the butler into a very large room that contained a huge grand piano, several oil paintings in massive gilt frames, and as eclectic a collection of furniture as he had ever seen. There were two or three antique Spanish pieces, a strikingly styled Plexiglas table, three modern sofas that appeared to be custom built, and a scattering of spindly French chairs. Harbizon concluded rapidly that the chairs were largely for show only; he could not imagine anyone wanting to sit on one of them. At Harkness' invitation, he seated himself on one of the sofas and nodded to Happs to take the opposite end.

Approximately three minutes later he looked up to see a woman coming into the room. As he got to his feet he kept his features composed with an effort. She was the fattest person he had ever seen. She could not have been more than five feet five, but she had to weigh more than three hundred pounds. Her head, thatched with carefully coiffured blond hair, was as flat and wide as a crabapple. Two features caught him: thick heavy lips that were painted a bright scarlet, and a pair of small black eyes that radiated hardness and distrust.

Her massive figure was made up of piled mounds of flesh that were visibly compressed by what must have been steel-ribbed corsets. The dress she had on was made of an expensive flowered material, but the designer had given up on subtlety. He had tried only to avoid total disgrace. It was wrapped around her like a tent, reaching halfway to her ankles, but even then it did not conceal the tree trunk legs that supported the whole gross body.

"Mrs. Lockheim?" Harbizon asked.

Without answering, the incredible woman eased herself down onto one end of a sofa that might have been specially built to hold her weight. Then her eyes glowed at him like live coals. "What do you want?" she asked in a voice that belonged in a fish market.

"I'm Lieutenant Harbizon, ma'am, from the police department. I would like to express our profound sympathy to you for what has just happened."

"Sympathy won't help a thing," she answered him. "My husband is dead, very suddenly, and everything is up in the air."

Harbizon detected no sorrow in her voice. She could have been speaking of the death of someone she had barely met and had not particularly liked. Perhaps, he thought, she was just case hardened and tough—the product of a hard childhood and possibly privation at one time or another. He wondered, because he could not help himself, if she had ever been normal-sized. Not slender, exactly, but able to pass muster as an attractive woman.

Still, with that face and those eyes, she must have been flint-hard from the beginning. "Are you aware of the nature of the accident?" he asked, probing for some sort of response.

He got more than he had hoped for. The woman leaned forward an inch or so, about as much as her body would allow, and her voice was suddenly armor plated. "Accident! Don't give me any of that crap. I was in my apartments upstairs, and I saw out the window. It was an explosion and that, mister, was no accident!"

She lifted her left arm and looked at a wrist watch fastened by gold links around a wrestler's forearm. Harbizon saw it as she turned her arm. It had a square face that was completely surrounded by diamonds. On each side of the dial there were square projections like a pair of crude wings, their faces glittered with more diamonds set as close together as the maker had been able to manage. Harbizon thought that it was probably worth a mint and also that it was the most vulgar thing he had ever seen. Her fingers were loaded with rings inset with still more diamonds, rubies, and two miniature carvings of Burmese jadeite. He had a sudden urge to find it all comical. With an effort he forced that thought out of his mind.

"Mrs. Lockheim," he tried again. "I don't want to distress you at such a time, but can you tell me if your husband had any known enemies?"

"Enemies? Everyone has enemies. Mr. Lockheim was very, very successful, and to be that you gotta make enemies. Maybe hundreds. I don't know."

"Has anyone, to your knowledge, threatened your husband's life recently?"

She lifted her huge shoulders and let them fall. "Maybe. People got mad at him at times, but I don't concern myself with that. My husband could take care of himself."

Harbizon carefully refrained from pointing out the fallacy in that. Instead, he watched as the little maid appeared once more, this time carrying a dessert plate. On it there was a large napoleon; whipped cream and chocolate syrup had been added. "I have a stomach condition," she said. "Something like an ulcer. I have to keep food on my stomach or it becomes very painful."

She picked up a fork, skimmed off a large lump of whipped cream, and put it in her mouth.

Harbizon saw no reason to prolong the interview. He had too many other pressing things to do. As he stood up, Happs dutifully followed his example. "Thank you for seeing us at such a difficult time, Mrs. Lockheim," he said.

The woman looked up at him, her jaws working on a chunk of the pastry. "Call me Gilda," she answered.

When Harbizon came outside, the fire department arson specialist was waiting for him. The two men did not bother to shake hands; it was not a social occasion. "What have you got, George?" Harbizon asked.

"So far, it was a bomb, of course, and the man who made it knew his business. It was expertly installed under the driver's seat on the frame, and then hooked up to the right-turn signal. That's a European trick, by the way, one of their special cuties. I did some thinking while you were inside. Lockheim drove home from the station and then went up right in front of his own place, fortunately where there was no one else to be hurt. I think that was intended.

On the route from the station to here there are two left turns, but none to the right until he reached his own driveway. If it had been wired the other way, the bomb would have gone off right in the heart of town."

"Thank God for small favors. Any idea about the type of bomb?"

"Not yet, because it could have been almost anything. The results are consistent with a neat plastic charge, but that's only a guess at the moment."

"So it comes down to one of two things—someone who didn't like Lockheim is an expert in the use of explosive devices, or else he knew how to get hold of a demolition man to do the job."

"That's how I see it too."

"And no chance of mistaken identity. That gold Caddie was one of the most conspicuous cars in the area."

"John, that could be it right there. Somebody who saw that big flashy car at the station every day let it get on his nerves . . ."

Harbizon cut him off. "I can't buy that as a motive for murder. Not premeditated, as this one was. This wasn't a simple killing, just a butcher knife in the chest sort of thing. This one was planned, and very carefully executed."

The arson specialist accepted that. "I'll go over the wreckage and fill you in by noon tomorrow. Unless you need it sooner."

"That'll be fine," Harbizon answered. He checked the scene once more. The body had been removed and the burned-out car was about to be towed away. A fireman was standing by to wash down the roadway. He got back into his car, called off the road blocks by radio, and then drove back to the police station. As he walked inside he met the deputy chief who actually filled a captain's role in the department structure. At the chief's invitation he went into his office and supplied all of the information that he had. The chief listened intently, without comment.

"It's too late tonight to do very much," Harbizon concluded, "but in the morning I'm going to start by checking for anyone who saw something being done to Lockheim's car. I don't have much hope. A lot of potential witnesses will deny seeing anything. And the man who planted that bomb was no fool."

"The FBI may be able to give us some help on known bombers."

"And after that, we can check on known enemies. His wife implied that he had some."

The deputy chief pushed back in his chair and pondered. "How much do you know about Lockheim?" he asked.

"Very little."

"Well, it depends, I guess, on how you view these things. He was a floor trader, a professional speculator on the stock exchange. So his career consisted in taking away other people's money, particularly the vulnerable small investors. Sometimes he lost, but usually he won. If you want to put it in harsh terms, he was a vulture."

"You could call that business acumen, couldn't you?" Harbizon asked.

"Yes, but so many of the so-called investors in the market don't want to gamble at all. A stockbroker somewhere recommends something and they buy it, hoping for a fair return and some eventual appreciation. But that can be like going for a beginner's swim in a pool of sharks. They don't know about the pros who are on the floor all the time for the sole purpose of skinning them. Lockheim undoubtedly broke a lot of people along the way. Some of them were other pros who understood the risks they were taking. A lot of them weren't."

Harbizon had never heard his deputy chief talk that way. "How much did he take you for?" he asked.

The chief made his voice deliberately unemotional. "It was my fault, John, and there's no one else to blame. I thought at the time that I was making a conservative investment, but it didn't really matter, because Betty got a scholarship anyway. She's a bright girl, you know—a lot brighter than her dad most of the time. Thank God my stupidity didn't hold her back. From what I know now, I take it that most of what I had went to add to Lockheim's profits. And I certainly wasn't the only one. So if you want to start tracking down his enemies, you may have quite a job ahead of you."

2

In the cooled, softly lighted atmosphere of the restaurant William San Marco felt himself to be very much at home. Because the location was well up into Westchester County, and on a carefully selected side road, it did not have the space problems it would have had on Manhattan Island. Consequently, the tables were comfortably separated one from another, and it was possible to talk without having total strangers on each side forced to listen to every word being said. He had careful plans laid for the young woman who was with him, and to bring them about with his usual *élan* he had been more than glad to drive up from the city. He liked the country anyway, up to a point.

He had called and reserved a window table even though he had known that it would be close to dark before he would arrive. It gave a certain feeling of insulation and, at the same time, a lack of confinement that the center tables could not avoid. The out of doors was there, available if needed.

The drinks on the table were of the elaborate tropical variety that were called by exotic names and served in hollowed-out pineapples. They tasted of rum and fruit juices, but there were other ingredients that upped their potential considerably under the guise of mild flavor. San Marco knew that very well. So did the girl who sat across from him, even though she had never been to that particular restaurant. "Um, nice," she said in appreciation. She delivered the line well, making it sound unsophisticated and quite sincere.

"I thought you might like it," San Marco said. "I believe in trying new things all the time. It makes life a helluva lot more interesting."

"Of course," she agreed as if the inner meaning of his remark had totally escaped her. "Anybody can do the same old things all of the time."

That answer pleased San Marco so much he decided at that moment to go whole hog on the dinner. If he spent four dollars on a drink, he expected it to get him four dollars and fifty cents' worth of results. That was the minimum. Some people he knew enjoyed spreading money around. It gratified their egos, and those who accepted it responded with all of the necessary flattery. When he spent any of his own money, every dollar was calculated. It was an overdeveloped sense, perhaps, but it was his stock in trade and he made it work for him. The good things in life all came from that semiprimitive instinct to protect himself at all times.

His decision made, he leaned forward with a winning casualness. "How about Chateaubriand for two?" he suggested. "They do it exceptionally well here."

His companion smiled as if she had taken a child-
ish delight in his having proposed the most expensive item on the already-costly menu. It had told her
something she had wanted to know, and the information warmed her as much as the unconventional
drink had done. "I'd just love it," she answered.

San Marco summoned the waiter with a manner
he had acquired only after careful practice in front
of a mirror. He tried to make it combine equal parts
of sophisticated youth, authority due to position, and
the irresistible force of a well-stuffed wallet. He
placed the order, specified lyonnaise potatoes and
fresh spinach on the side, and added that they would
have coffee later. He overdid it very slightly, but not
enough, he was sure, to do anything but impress the
woman on the other side of the table.

She considered him a clown, but for the purpose
she had in mind, she was willing to make
allowances.

San Marco was three weeks under fifty years of
ago. The anguish of his fiftieth birthday was something he had decided to circumvent by fixing in his
mind that he was actually forty-seven and by never
allowing himself to abandon that illusion for a moment. He did not like being forty-seven either, but
he felt that he could defeat his numerical age by
looking and acting as though he were still in his
romantic thirties. He never visualized himself as
anything other than romantic. He had even chosen
his name with that in view. And he had certainly
made out with the women. There his money had

been of great help, but he had never paid for it, not directly. Women wanted him, and that was the most important thing in his life.

Of course he had done his part. He had spent a fortune on clothes, cars, and cosmetic advantages. In fact, he was remarkably youthful looking, and the hair transplant had been a considerable success.

As the dinner progressed he kept up the brilliant conversation that he knew would overwhelm the young woman he had chosen for his next conquest. She was something very special. If she proved to be as good as he dared to hope, he was prepared to take care of her for a while. He had a recently vacated apartment available and few additional arrangements would be needed. The apartment was well chosen and also well buried in his business expense records. He took a secret delight in the knowledge that he was also taking it off his income tax.

As soon as the dessert had been served, and everyone in the dining room knew that they were having cherries jubilee, he went into his well-rehearsed speech. "You know, Marcia, you can laugh at me if you like, but just having this dinner with you means a lot more to me than you might think. You're not an ordinary girl, you know."

He had never found a woman who wouldn't swallow that line.

She flashed him a smile with slightly pursed lips and bedroom eyes. "I think you're assuming too much," she told him. Inwardly she knew that it was true. She wasn't an ordinary girl as far as he was concerned. When he found that out, it might be the biggest shock he had ever known.

He picked up a spoon and began to toy with his cherries. "Look, Marcia, this is the first time that we've had dinner together, but I don't think it will be the last. I certainly hope not."

"Thank you," she responded.

"I'd like to get to know you a lot better. Do you have any terribly serious commitment that would prevent it?" He knew, of course, that she didn't.

She pretended to think for a moment. "No, I don't think so. Not right at the moment. Of course . . ."

"We'll cross that bridge when we come to it. You told me that you write feature pieces to order, but that you don't have an assignment right now. Perhaps I can help. I know a lot of people."

"You must, I know, but I don't know how you've done it all. Bill, how old are you?"

He didn't think at all. "I'm older than I look, Marcia. I might as well admit that right away. I'm forty-five."

She looked at him as if she couldn't believe what she had heard. She had half thought of sending him a birthday card in three weeks' time, but thank the Lord she had avoided that blunder. "I'm amazed," she declared. "I thought you were in your late thirties—possibly forty, but certainly no more than that."

He smiled what he considered his boyish best. "At least I'm not over the hill; not by a long ways yet."

"You'd never have to tell any woman that," she flattered.

It was going so splendidly he congratulated himself that he was combining both youth and experience in his best performance to date. Forty-five was older than he wanted to be, but it was true—he sometimes looked at himself a certain way in the mirror and he did look as though he were in his late thirties. A good James Bond age.

"I'm going to declare myself," he said, skipping by instinct much that he had so carefully prepared. "I am single again, at last, and I have the income to provide practically everything that anyone could want, but I'm not in the market for anybody. If you'll let me, I'd like to give you the time of your life for a while—until one of us says 'when.' And I can tell you right now, it won't be me." That certainly ought to be clear. Obviously, this was a girl who had been around enough to understand him, and if she proved to be really good in the sack, then he might keep it up for a considerable while. She was an exciting wench.

"Let me think about it," she said.

For the sake of the impression it would make on her, he left a very generous tip and was most gentlemanly as he made his way out. That was a part he had learned to perfection.

Outside the air was remarkably soft and warm. The very large parking lot held only a few vehicles. It was an off night. He handed a dollar to the parking attendant and said, "I'll pick it up myself."

He made a little ceremony of putting her into the huge black Cadillac, and then turned the key on and

lowered the windows, letting the inviting air inside.
"Can we drive a little before we go back?" he asked.

"Of course."

That was the key response—the implied consent.
He had it made, he knew it. Dizzy with delight at his
own virtuosity, he slipped the car into gear and
turned up the road. He kept the speed moderate so
as not to upset her by blowing her hair too much;
women were funny that way. Within three or four
minutes he had the road to himself except for one
other car well behind him that showed no disposi-
tion to catch up and pass. If the other driver wanted
to, he would let him. He was in that generous a
mood.

They reached the spot in twelve minutes' time.
He stopped at the place he knew and without the
weakness of making an excuse turned to his companion. He rested his hand very gently on her shoulder in the darkness and became as tender as he could
simulate. She came to him, not too eagerly, but in a
way that showed she was a real woman with all her
internal fires banked, but burning. He kissed her
forehead, and when she responded ever so slightly,
he went into his carefully developed routine.

The only awkward moment was getting her into
the back seat, but he managed it. When she came
with him his last doubt was erased and his loins
were bursting with anticipation and eagerness.
Presently she was his in a way that was all that he
could hope for in the relatively confined space.
When he entered her she guided him in and then

began a little motion of her own that made the blood pound in his veins. She was fantastic!

He paid the price of his overanxiousness and reached his climax almost at once. With a sigh he let his weight sink on top of her while he recovered his breath. For years he had kept a mental roster of names, and he made a small ceremony of adding her to it. One more full point advance in his impressive personal score.

"Good evening."

The voice, almost in his ear, hit him like a thunderclap. For a bare moment he was unable to move. He had never been so startled in his life.

His mind was racing. A cop, it had to be a cop. Consenting adults, that's what they were, and fornication wasn't an offense any more. Embarrassing, hell for the girl, but she'd live through it. After all, she'd been had a good many times before.

Then he felt a piece of cold metal press against his forehead and terror flooded him until he couldn't even jibber.

"Don't move," the voice commanded. "Stay exactly the way that you are."

He couldn't have moved for anything. It was all that he could do to keep breathing. Only his mind worked, and because he was used to tight corners he managed to speak. "My wallet's on the front seat. Help yourself. I'm insured." He started to rise.

"I said, don't move!"

He froze in compliance, despite the total awkwardness of his position.

The hard steel was still against his head. "Now, Mr. San Marco, you've come to the end of the road. You have just screwed somebody for the last time."

"No!" he shrieked. The sound was still in his throat when the first silenced bullet hit him. He never felt the second.

The call that came into the state police reported that there was an hysterical woman screaming in the middle of the roadway. The informant refused to give his ID, but he had taken the trouble to call the mobile operator from the phone in his car.

In response Trooper Stephen Petit was dispatched to the location. As soon as he was in the vicinity, Petit began to cruise slowly, using his movable spotlight and with his roof lights on. A quarter of a mile further on he found her, sitting by the side of the road, sobbing, and obviously in some form of shock. He stopped his car beside her and went to her assistance in his most considerate manner. "Can I help you, miss?" he said.

The girl replied by grabbing him savagely around the legs and hanging on with desperation. Petit let her stay that way for a good thirty seconds before he did anything about it. Then he bent down and gently pried her arms free. "What happened?" he inquired, keeping his voice calm and soothing.

The young woman began to babble, but he could not understand what she was trying to say. He did grasp that she wanted him to go back in the direction from which he had come; she kept pointing that way. He eased her gently into the car, turned around, and began to drive very slowly toward the north. The girl was still inarticulate, but she continued to point ahead. As he drove, Petit picked up his microphone and in careful language, because the girl could hear him, he reported the probable need for medical help.

He had just finished speaking when the young woman clutched his sleeve and pointed toward a turn-off on the left-hand side. He took it at once without hesitation. He had turned his roof lights off but kept his movable spot on so that he could scan the area as he went.

Within a short two hundred feet he found the black sedan. After sweeping it with his spotlight he got out carefully, his weapon at the ready. He approached the semihidden car with full caution, and when he was close enough, he looked inside. As soon as he had done so, he hurried back to his own vehicle and reported what he had found.

The response took a little while because of the location, but in not much more than fifteen minutes four other vehicles had arrived, including an ambulance with an intern aboard. The young woman, who was still incoherent, was turned over to the intern's care while the police personnel began a systematic investigative procedure. A trooper armed with a camera popped innumerable flash bulbs as he recorded the whole scene, both close-up and at a moderate distance, from every available angle. The doctor, having quieted his patient, examined what remained of William San Marco and pronounced him dead without hesitation. The victim was not a pretty sight, but policemen and medics in the greater New York area were all too familiar with violent death, and to some extent they had gotten used to it.

The ID of the dead man was called in together with a request for the NYPD to supply as much information about him as its computers could print out from what was already stored in their memories. It was close to daybreak before everything that could be done at the scene had been completed, the body removed, and the car towed away to the police garage. Within a comparatively short time the road would once more be in normal use. Of the hundreds who would drive past during the morning to come, none would see any evidence that something out of the ordinary had taken place. And if they did happen to hear about the murder on one of the news broadcasts, they wouldn't particularly care.

After the shifts had changed, a considerable readout on San Marco came in from the New York Police Department. He had once been charged with rape, but the young woman involved had changed her story and withdrawn the complaint. He had had a considerable record of traffic offenses, but no warrants were outstanding. He had given his occupation as "financial specialist," a designation that covered a very wide area. He had also been twice divorced and had been named in another action.

Sergeant Charles Dietrich, the homicide investigator assigned to the case, probed deeper and came out almost at once with two interesting items. First, the victim had been employed as a "specialist" on the floor of the stock exchange; secondly, his true name was not William San Marco. He had been born just short of fifty years before, in the Bronx, as Moshe Feldman.

Sergeant Dietrich had never put any of his own money into the market, and he did not know very much about the way it operated. To find out precisely what the dead man had done, he called on a stockbroker he knew and asked for a full explanation with nothing omitted. He still did not have an inkling of a motive. He could think of several possibilities, but he had no evidence to support any one of them.

"Since this is a police matter, I'll give it to you the way it really is," the broker began. "The stock exchange puts out the idea that it is a trading facility. In fact, if you go up on the balcony you can see an unbelievably juvenile display that shows how a farmer in the Midwest, who has some stock he doesn't want, sells it, through the exchange of course, to a sweet old lady in New Hampshire who just happens to want precisely what he has and who finds the price to her liking. That's bullshit. What really happens is this. Each stock admitted for trading has what is called a specialist who handles all of the transactions concerning that particular company. A specialist may handle two or three stocks, but seldom more than that. So if you want to sell stock in the XYZ Company, you sell it to the specialist. If you want to buy some, you buy it from him. And he sets the price in both instances."

"In other words," the sergeant said, "he runs the only game in town."

"You've got it. When the market is going up, he may take his stock up with it, or he may keep the price down for a while. He has a lot of leeway. Without going into all of the details about shorting, trading against the box, and other maneuvers, he usually manages to keep things in hand so that he comes out with a substantial profit. Sometimes he will get caught, but the specialists are sharp—they have to be—and you won't catch them in a corner very often."

"And it's the investors who pay him," the sergeant suggested.

"Correct. In many different ways. Just for example, John Doe buys a thousand shares of XYZ at thirty-five, and then to insure himself against too severe a loss, he puts in what is called a stop order. That is, he authorizes his broker to sell the stock for him at a lower figure, but not too much lower. So John Doe puts in his stop order at thirty-one. If it reaches that figure, he will be sold out at a loss of four thousand dollars, plus commission, but that's all he can lose. Sounds great, doesn't it? But that stop order goes to the specialist who knows that he can buy a thousand shares of XYZ at thirty-one. So, if he wants to, he can usually manage to take the price down just to the sellout figure. The broker holding the stock follows orders and sells. The specialist picks it up and then lets the price rise again. Of course, he can't bother to do that every time, but in the smaller stocks where there is not too much trading action, it can be a nice gimmick for him. The average customers don't know this. To them the stop-loss order looks like a very good idea, and under some circumstances it is."

"Just suppose that the stockholder simply decides to sell if the stock reaches a certain figure and then keeps his eyes open?" Dietrich asked.

"That's doing it the smart way, of course, but few actually do go that route. The stock reaches the sell-out figure, and they don't have the discipline to dump. They hang in there figuring that it will turn around soon and they won't have to swallow a bad loss. And down it may go until they become alarmed, at which point it's too late. Also, how many people have nothing to do but sit and watch the market all day? The professionals do, of course, that's one reason why they make out."

For another half hour the sergeant gathered information and then closed his notebook to leave. At the door he turned back with one more question. "I forgot to ask," he said. "What was the stock that San Marco represented?"

The broker didn't know that offhand, but a single phone call produced the information. "Sphinx Wire and Cable," he reported.

3

Lieutenant John Harbizon was practically prepared to sell his soul for one good cooperative witness. Everywhere he turned he ran into the New York syndrome that has as its basic creed, *Don't Get Involved*.

No one at the railroad station was able to, or would, tell him a thing. One man recalled that quite often car repair people came to the parking lot and worked on one or the other of the cars there. It wasn't the railroad's business. The lot was provided as a convenience with no liability of any kind attached. Someone might have been on the lot, working on Lockheim's car, but he hadn't noticed. Furthermore, he couldn't remember any one in particular who came to the lot. He had other work to do.

Harbizon knew that it would be futile to check with the available garages. The wiring job on Lockheim's car hadn't been done by any repairman in Boylesport.

The report from the arson investigator gave him nothing new that he could use. The explosive charge had been put under the driver's seat, not in the gas tank as might have been expected. It had been a professional job all the way, with the added note, in case the lieutenant had forgotten, that the turn-signal trick was a European invention.

Patiently, carefully, Harbizon built up his file. He was not a man easily discouraged. If it came simply, that was fine. If it did not, he was prepared to do whatever was necessary the hard way.

When five days had elapsed, and the memorial services had been concluded, he braced himself for an ordeal and went once more to call on Mrs. Gilda Lockheim. As before, he was kept waiting until it suited her to present herself. When she at last waddled in, Harbizon rose to his feet like a humble petitioner. The sight of her in a pink pants suit was almost more than he could handle. He could not imagine what had persuaded her to wear a thing like that, which, if anything, mercilessly emphasized her elephantine proportions. He guessed that she had issued a peremptory order concerning style and color and then had left the defenseless designer no choice but to commit artistic harakiri. She sank onto one end of the same sofa and fixed him with her hard, glinting eyes. "I don't know a damn thing more than I did last time," she greeted him. "What does your wife call you?"

He saw no need to tell her that like so many other policemen he was divorced. "John," he answered.

"All right, John, get on with it."

He began on a carefully calculated soft note. "I

sincerely hope that Mr. Lockheim left you well provided for."

She gulped the bait like a frog snaring one more fly. "You could say so. I inherit this place and about ten million after taxes, the way it looks now. With what I've already got, I should be comfortable."

"I sincerely hope so," he lied easily. Privately he thought it would be wonderful if she were compelled to go to work somewhere. "Mrs. Lockheim— Gilda—I'm making a complete investigation of your husband's death. If I'm successful, I'll catch the man or woman who was responsible. Right now I'm anxious to get every detail that I can."

"Somebody blew his ass off, that's all there is to it." Her voice held no trace of emotion. Apparently realizing that, she added, "He was a good provider."

"Obviously. Gilda, can you tell me how he got his start?"

His subject heaved herself into a fresh position. "Hell yes, I gave it to him. When we were married, it was my dough that set him up. He was young then, but smart and already he had some good connections. So I staked him enough to get on the exchange and have some capital to work with. It was a business deal, strictly, and we signed papers over it. He wanted it that way, he said for tax reasons. He made money almost right from the beginning."

"Gilda, did your husband ever do any other work?"

"Nat? No, he wasn't fitted for it. He was a speculator, but a damn good one. He used to tell me that he let others do the sweating, but when he was in school he was a theater usher once for about three weeks. Something about having to take a job for that long to get his degree."

"What was his degree in?"

"Investments and banking, I think. I'm not sure."

For a half hour longer, Harbizon asked his questions and for the most part received candid answers. But with them came very little information that he could use. He asked the proper things, but most of the time his subject simply didn't know, or at least that's what she said. He did confirm that the relationship between the dead man and his wife had been passive for some time, but since Gilda had held the purse strings to a considerable degree, a separation had never been mentioned. Harbizon thanked her and left.

On the way back he laid out his next moves. First, get a list, if he could, of those persons who had lost substantially to Lockheim during the past six months—a year if the data could be located. Then he would check that list for any persons who had been in service and who had had demolition or other explosive experience.

Although it didn't help matters very much, it was evident to him that whoever the killer might be, he knew a lot about the stock market. The FBI had once examined two million pieces of handwriting looking for one suspect and had found him. Compared to that, his job should be relatively easy.

Also, the killer might be satisfied having taken his

revenge on Lockheim, or he might not. He resolved
to make a careful check of every reported homicide,
or possibly related incident, that might involve a
prominent stock market personality. Or a broker.
That was a pretty good bet—a broker who had led a
victim into Lockheim's fly trap might have good
cause to be worried. There was a lot of work to be
done.

When he reached his office, there was a note on
his desk to call Sergeant Charles Dietrich of the state
police. A direct Westchester County number was
supplied.

When he had Dietrich on the line he identified
himself and then waited.

Dietrich came right to the point. "I understand
that you're handling the Lockheim killing."

"That's right. What can I do for you?"

"We've just had one up here that may be related.
The MO is entirely different, the victim was shot at
close range in his car—while he was humping a girl,
as a matter of fact."

"What a way to die!"

"Right, and it blew the girl's mind. The reason I
called you—the deceased was involved in the stock
market. He was a floor specialist, if that means anything to you."

"Not at the moment, but go on. Who's the
victim?"

"He was known as William San Marco but his
real name was Moshe Feldman. Another one, I take
it, who changed his name for business reasons."

Harbizon thought. "I think we ought to get together," he said. "I can think of two possibilities that might link these crimes together."

"So can I, and I don't like the second one one damn bit. I think the stock market angle is a good one, and that's what I'm following up at the moment. Incidentally, our killing was pretty tricky—not as simple as it sounds."

Harbizon reacted. "Fill me in," he requested.

"Our man was shot with an undersized bullet. You know the trick—you take, say, a thirty-eight cartridge and take out the bullet. In its place you put a smaller one, or possibly shave the original. It only works at short range, because it cuts way down on the accuracy, but it effectively prevents any kind of a ballistics test. As it is, I can't even say what caliber of gun was used."

"Was it dumdummed?"

"Good guess, it was. Whoever did the job isn't a casual killer. I'm running a check on all of the recent boyfriends of the witness and it's a pretty full list. If one of those guys was pissed off, he might get a gun and shoot San Marco, but he wouldn't go to the trouble of that trick shot. And he probably wouldn't know how."

"All right, Dietrich, here's something for you. The mechanic who did the job here was a pro and a cute one—probably European trained. Definitely not an amateur. Let's get together."

"I'll be with you in an hour," Dietrich said.

* * *

Harbizon welcomed his guest with a cup of bitter coffee that came out of a machine, and they spent five minutes in professional small talk. When that was over he knew the quality of the man who had come to see him and approved. Dietrich knew the homicide business; no doubt of that. After that he listened while he laid out his case. He saw no point of real similarity. The stock market connection was the best bet, plus the remote possibility that he still held in the back of his mind. When Dietrich had finished, he gave him a briefing on his own case, including the details that had not been made public. The turn-signal gimmick was one of them. The witness who had seen the explosion had not made that connection, or if he had, he had been careful not to mention it.

Dietrich listened with total attention. "Now we have two things," he said. "Both were stock market profiteers, parasites of a kind. A lot of people might have reason to hate them, but most of those who lost their money to them would never know their names. Or even that they existed. I had a broker brief me. Secondly, we have evidence that the killer in both cases was a genuine pro, someone who knows his business thoroughly."

"There's one other thought," Harbizon said.

"I know, lieutenant, and God forbid. Both victims were Jewish; it could just be . . ."

Harbizon kept his unbroken calm. "We've had the SLA, the Weathermen, and a number of other violent revolutionary groups. A Nazi kind of thing could be the answer. There are some organizations around."

"I know. We have files on them, of course, and the FBI has all kinds of information. I don't think that's it, because I presume that a good percentage of Wall Street operators are Jewish. And two out of two is a pretty small percentage."

Harbizon had an inspiration. "By any chance," he asked, "do you happen to know, yet, the name of any stocks that San Marco handled?"

"Yes. So far only one, but he specialized in it. Sphinx Wire and Cable."

"Eureka!" Harbizon snapped back. "That's the stock that Lockheim was involved in. I distinctly remember that name coming up."

Dietrich was elated and allowed it to show. "Out of eighteen hundred stocks they were both on that one. There's the connection. I won't buy a coincidence."

"Neither will I. What do you say that we hit the stock exchange together in the morning?"

"You're on," Dietrich answered.

Three men were waiting for them when they arrived at the stock exchange. With careful formality everyone shook hands, then the small party settled into a conference room that had been designed for groups of from twelve to twenty. That made it possible for the five men present to gather at one end of the long central table with a suggestion of confidential rapport.

Harbizon opened his notebook and wrote at the top of a fresh page the names of the three men: Marcus, Fellini, and Stone. As he did so, his colleague from the state police opened the meeting.

"Gentlemen, Lieutenant Harbizon and I are heading up the investigation into the deaths of Mr. Nathan Lockheim and Mr. William San Marco, respectively. We know that both men were active on the floor of the exchange, and we feel that the killings may very well be related."

Marcus cut in quickly. "I understand what you are saying, sergeant, but simply because both men traded on the exchange floor it doesn't follow that their deaths are necessarily in any way connected."

Opposite the name "Marcus," Harbizon wrote *lawyer.* He looked up to see Dietrich looking at him, clearly putting a silent question.

He answered it affirmatively. "Gentlemen, you probably know this already, but both victims were associated in the trading of the stock of Sphinx Wire and Cable. That narrows the matter considerably."

The man called Fellini looked worried for a bare moment, then he spoke. "That certainly appears significant, gentlemen, and since this is a police investigation, I'll be completely candid with you on another point. I have informed myself in both of these killings insofar as the press reports permit. I know that Mr. San Marco was shot while . . . in the company of a young lady. Strictly not for publication, he had a reputation as a ladies' man. You understand what I'm driving at."

Opposite his name Harbizon wrote *PR*.

"We've already determined that, Mr. Fellini," Dietrich replied smoothly. "Two of our detectives are at work right now exploring that angle. Lieutenant Harbizon is also checking on the private life of Mr. Lockheim to see what may be significant there."

The one named Stone shifted slightly, but did not speak. John Harbizon addressed him immediately. "In the confidence of this meeting," he said to the austere, white-haired man across from him, "if you can assist me there, I would appreciate it."

Stone took hardly a second before he replied, but it was enough for Harbizon. "I dislike very much discussing the private affairs of our members, but in view of the circumstances I will tell you, totally in confidence, that Lockheim was tied to his wife by legal commitments in addition to marriage. She is not an attractive woman, as you certainly already know. He did have a discreet lady companion whom he had maintained for some time. Apart from that, he was very circumspect in his personal affairs. I doubt if this has any bearing on your investigation. He provided very generously for his wife, and the other lady involved, I happen to know, was most satisfied with the arrangement. I understand that she has no relatives."

Harbizon nodded his understanding and made a note. Opposite Stone's name he wrote *brass*.

Fellini cleared his throat, "Er, gentlemen, I do have something to tell you, but I'm somewhat hesitant. However"—he paused, pretending a moment's confusion—"you understand that the exchange is just that. We provide a trading facility and the necessary support functions, basically that's all. Many fortunes have been made here, and, unquestionably, some have been lost. But usually by investors who were not prudent in their selections or who, frankly, were speculating. Within the past ten days Mr. Lockheim received a letter, here at the exchange, from what appears to be a mentally deranged person. However, it does contain a death threat directed against him. Mr. Lockheim turned it in to us, and our security people are investigating."

"Not the NYPD?" Dietrich asked.

Fellini shrugged. "Gentlemen, if we turned over every crank letter we receive to the New York Police, they wouldn't have time for anything else."

"Of course," Marcus added, "if anything were to come in that we had reason to believe was a genuine police matter, we would report it immediately."

"I understand," Harbizon said. "Incidentally, gentlemen, Sergeant Dietrich and I have both been seconded to the NYPD for the purpose of this investigation. That's quite customary in cases of this kind. Now I would like to see the letter."

Fellini looked at Stone who nodded his head a half inch. The PR man opened a folder and passed the note across. Harbizon took it, checked the envelope, and then read the brief letter inside. When he had done so, he passed it to Dietrich and remained quiet while his colleague digested the piece of evidence. When he had finished Dietrich issued an order. "I'd like to have your security people fill us in on anything they have on this letter to date. Since it passed through the mail, it's federal. However, as I read it, it is more an expression of anger. The phrase 'it would be better if you were dead' isn't precisely a death threat."

"Quite possibly not," Stone said. "But we thought you ought to be told."

"Certainly," Harbizon responded. "Now a question at this point. How many letters like this come in here, on the average?"

Fellini looked once more at Stone who, in turn, was looking at Marcus. The lawyer answered. "Not very many, actually, because few members of the public have any idea who our floor traders are, or the names of the specialists who handle specific securities."

"But they can find out if they want to?"

Marcus hesitated. "Yes, I would say that they could if they wanted to make the effort."

Dietrich had a question. "Since you are already investigating this letter from"—he checked the name once more—"Daniel Sisler, I presume you can tell me the amount of his loss in the Sphinx Wire and Cable stock."

"Well, I'm not sure . . ."

"About eight thousand dollars," Stone cut in, "which, to a little man, could be quite a lot."

"I see. Mr. Stone, understanding that a double homicide is involved, and we have to consider the possibility of more if we don't stop this immediately, would you say that this particular stock had been manipulated?"

Stone did not blink an eye. "A pitcher manipulates a baseball when he throws it toward the plate. The term is very catholic. It is a matter of record that that particular security did have some rather dramatic fluctuations during the past several months. But there is no evidence whatever of any wrongdoing in that. When people buy, a stock goes up. When they sell, it goes down. Substantially it's as simple as that."

"Superficially," Harbizon responded, "that's true, of course, but if there is a material change in interest rates, for instance, that can affect the market quite drastically, isn't that true?"

Stone did not move a muscle. "Perfectly true, lieutenant, but I call your attention to the fact that the change in interest rates normally influences buying and selling and that, in turn, has an effect on prices."

In his notebook Harbizon underlined the name *Stone*. Then he stood up. "Thank you for your cooperation, gentlemen," he said. "I'm sure that we will be meeting again soon."

Outside the conference room there were two fairly young men waiting. As soon as Harbizon appeared they closed in on him. "Lieutenant Harbizon?" one of them asked. He could have been thirty-five. Harbizon's first impression of him was of slightly bug eyes and a complexion two shades lighter than it should have been. He wondered instantly if the man had been in prison.

"Yes," he answered. "What do you want?"

"My name is Bert Schneider, *Amalgamated News*. This is my partner, Gene Burroughs."

The light went on. *Amalgamated News* was new, aggressive, and making waves, even in New York.

"Burroughs and Schneider," Harbizon repeated. "I know the byline."

"Please, lieutenant, Schneider and Burroughs. Otherwise they abbreviate it BS. You see the point."

"I do. My colleague, Sergeant Dietrich, state police."

The two reporters shook hands. Burroughs, Harbizon noted, wore elevator shoes of a very expensive make. His suit was much better cut than was required for his job. A second look at Schneider confirmed that he was wearing what appeared to be a twenty-five- or thirty-dollar tie. He made an easy deduction that the well-known investigative reporters commanded pay checks commensurate with their considerable fame—or notoriety. "How did you ID me?" he asked.

Schneider answered him. "We learned you were on the case from the Boylesport Police. As soon as we had your name, we got a mug shot out of the morgue. We also read about the jewel heists that you cracked. Congratulations."

Burroughs took the conversational ball like a pivoting second baseman. "We're working on a new series about the stock market. It's been done before, of course, but during this last year there's been a major increase in stories of financial wrongdoing, a lot of them dealing with stock transactions."

Stone had disappeared, but Fellini was still present. He came forward with his hands half raised, palms toward the reporters. "Gentlemen, please. I told you only last week that we would cooperate fully with you, but harassing these officers at this time . . ."

The words were fine, but the way they were spoken said something else entirely. Harbizon caught the difference clearly, and it riled him. Also, the people of Boylesport, for the most part, were very conscious of press coverage—of the kind they approved. "We've got another appointment," Dietrich said, then he caught Harbizon's reaction. "But we can spare you five minutes."

"That'll do it," Burroughs said. "Let's go outside."

The interview was conducted in the police car that Dietrich had provided. Schneider opened a notebook, a gold Cross pen in his hand. "Look," he said, "to save time, we already know about the connection between the deaths of Lockheim and San Marco. That last is a phony name, by the way."

"What connection?" Harbizon asked.

"How did you find out?" Dietrich added. The two speeches almost overlapped.

"They both dealt in Sphinx Wire and Cable. Lockheim was the trader, San Marco the specialist. They worked hand-in-glove. A couple of savvy parasites." Schneider seemed to savor the words.

"Aren't you being a little hard on them?" Dietrich asked.

Burroughs was ready with an answer. "San Marco was a cocksman: He only beat a rape charge by buying the girl off, and that isn't all that he had to pay. When he was seventeen he was up for manslaughter—traffic accident—but he beat it and managed to get the record sealed. Juvenile. Legally yes, but his little girlfriend was pregnant at the time."

That was one Harbizon had missed, but he gave no indication. "What do you want from us?" he asked.

"First, any suspects?"

"None in custody at this time."

"How about the girl Marco was having when he got it?"

"Our next step. We haven't talked to her yet."

Schneider took over. It was an effective technique—one man questioned while the other formulated his questions to follow. "Are both of you going to stay on the case?"

Dietrich answered, "Until we're told to stop."

"And what might cause that?"

"The right suspect in custody, with all necessary evidence to prove his guilt."

"Aren't you the Sergeant Dietrich who solved the Fleisch killing about three years ago?"

"I was on the team. It was a combined effort."

"As I recall, the suspect confessed."

"Not in words, but he shot himself just before we got to him."

Burroughs was warmed up and ready. "Do you

believe that the fact that both of the murdered men were in the stock market is a significant factor in the two cases?"

"That's a possibility, certainly," Harbizon answered. "We intend to check out all of the leads we can uncover."

"One more. In general terms, are you aware of the number of major stories dealing with stock market frauds and manipulations that have appeared recently in the *Wall Street Journal*?"

Harbizon had a dead safe answer for that. "I don't read the *Wall Street Journal*. Gentlemen, that's all."

The reporters got out of the car and took the trouble to express their thanks as they left. When they were out of range Dietrich commented, "They're sharp."

"Yes, I agree. But we didn't give them very much."

Dietrich pressed his lips together in grim irony. "Just how much did we have to give them?" he asked. "Let's go and see the girl."

The building on the West Side was in the sixties not too far from Broadway. It had once had a moderate dignity, but that had been stolen by spray cans of black paint that had defaced it with words and symbols against which it had no defense. The few steps up to the door might have been scrubbed during some long gone decade, but now they were hopelessly overlaid with dirt that seemed to have penetrated deep into the stone. It was four stories tall and neither man had to be told that there was no elevator.

The lobby, such as it was, had a broken tile floor and a worn-out door that still hung on its hinges and made a pretext of protecting the interior. A small row of mail slots was on the right-hand side; a few had cut-off cards stuck in their name slots, all of them were decorated with more rust than paint. There was an odor of stale tobacco smoke and a suggestion of urine. Dietrich checked his notebook and then pushed one of the buttons that had no name card to identify it. After some delay the remote latch of the inner door buzzed.

The girl who called herself Marcia Churchill lived on the third floor. The steps up were steep and hard. There were fittings still in place that had once held carpeting, but they had been unemployed for a long procession of dreary years. The neighborhood had gone down, Harbizon concluded, to the point where the landlord refused to spend anything that wasn't essential on his building. He would still have tenants.

Although it was approaching noon, Marcia was wrapped in a thin pink robe that was faded from many washings. She had combed her hair and had used some cosmetics, but even in the less-than-adequate light of her doorway the signs of accelerating age and hard urban living marked her. As soon as Dietrich had introduced himself and Harbizon, she admitted them listlessly and planted herself in a worn chair for the inevitable recounting of her story.

The front room was small and looked out over the street: It was a toss up whether it was worth looking through the window or not. There was a fake fireplace that had once been a half attempt at elegance; now it admitted itself to be a fraud and earned its Lebenstraum by displaying a small assortment of pictures and a stuffed animal that had a thin veneer of plush.

"I've been waiting for you," she said. "I knew you'd come, sooner or later. I can't tell you a lot."

There was an undertone to that that Harbizon caught, a fighting against nonentity, a desire not to be just another police interviewee. It didn't take him a second to shape his response to it. "Miss Churchill," he said, "we both realize that you've been through a frightful experience. We appreciate your receiving us here in your home."

It was her home, to a point, as long as she paid the rent promptly and accepted the inevitable increases that were periodically imposed. But it was drained dry of pride. It was a small area in which to live from day to day, from week to week, until something broke, one way or the other.

Dietrich followed him perfectly; he said nothing but he radiated sympathy and understanding. And, as Harbizon had hoped, the girl fell for it. "It's nice to be treated like a lady," she responded. "I know what you're after. Do you think that if I give you all that I can, you could go easy on me? The wrong publicity could kill me right now."

"Answer two questions first," Harbizon countered. "First, do you know who killed Mr. San Marco?"

"No."

"As far as you know, did you have anything whatever to do with his death?"

"No."

John Harbizon sat back and visibly relaxed his manner. "In that case, I think we can leave it that two gentlemen know how to treat a lady."

She drank up the implied flattery like a starving kitten with a saucer of milk. "You're all right," she said. "Are you sure you're cops?"

Without comment both men displayed credentials. She shook her head. "The smart thing is never to talk to cops, but I want out. I want to get free of this thing as fast as I can."

"Perhaps," Dietrich suggested, "if you do give us all that you can this time, it may not be necessary for us, or anyone else, to come back." Harbizon gave his temporary partner a strong vote of confidence. The state police sergeant knew his business. And, essentially, he had spoken the truth.

The girl tilted her head back and stretched her arms out along the back of her chair. When she spoke, she could have been addressing the ceiling. "You can look me up, I know it, so I'll save you the trouble. My real name isn't Marcia Churchill, I'm east European, and I come from Pittsburgh. My parents were immigrants. I'm thirty-four and trying my damndest to pass for twenty-six or seven. Once I had ideas about a career, but that's all blown now.

All I'm after is a man to take care of me and get me out of this." Her gesture included the room and, by implication, everything about the apartment, the building, and the street outside. "For a while I was damn good looking, but I blew it and married the man of my dreams. There are different kinds of dreams."

"Such as nightmares," Harbizon suggested.

"Right. Let's skip the details. I'm not a call girl. I've never been. You know I was getting laid when San Marco, if you want to call him that, was shot. So there's no point in being coy about it. If a man can do something for me, he gets something in return. I don't think that's too bad."

"How long had you known Mr. San Marco?" Dietrich asked. His voice was gentle.

"Not too long. But long enough to have looked him up." She shifted her position and looked at Dietrich directly. "Let's lay it on the line. I can pass as good looking, and young, for maybe another year or two. After that, who knows? I found out that he has a plush apartment over on the East Side where he puts up his mistresses. None of them last too long, but in the beginning he likes to play the bigshot. I know the girl he had a year ago. She told me that I might be able to make a play for him and get him to keep me. The ride might be good for six months if I really worked at it. Meanwhile, I could built up a nest egg. There's only one cushion that will soften the bumps in life, and that's cash. Green, beautiful money. I need some, badly. He was a fifty-year-old egotistic freak, but he had the money, and he was determined to spend some of it on a girl who would tell him that she couldn't believe that he was forty-five and pretend that no other man in the world could screw her so magnificently. That's why I let him have me that night. If he bought it, and I was pretty sure that he would, then I had my six months of comfort and whatever I could gather on the side—legally of course."

Harbizon nodded. "I don't blame you a damn bit for trying," he said, and half meant it. The apartment he was in would have driven him out of his mind in a week's time. "Miss Churchill, how did you meet Mr. San Marco?"

"The girl I told you about set it up. She made it look accidental."

"She wasn't jealous?"

She shook her head vigorously. "No way. She had had her ride, and there was nothing more there for her. You see, this man was an egomaniac, he had to have new girls all the time to convince himself that he was young and dashing, and irresistible to women. He'd had his face lifted and a hair transplant—my girlfriend told me all about it."

"However, he was apparently a good stock trader."

She waved a hand in the air. "I don't know anything about that, except that he did have a lot of money. And he told me that he was making it hand over fist, but a lot of guys give you that line. Helen, that's my girlfriend, told me something else. He liked to appear to be splurging, but he never spent a dime unless he thought he was getting something for it worth at least fifteen cents—or more."

"Marcia, just for the record, I'd like your girl-friend's name." Harbizon had been holding that question, waiting until the moment was right.

"I didn't want to tell you that."

"Probably we won't need to talk to her at all," Harbizon said, trying to sound as though he meant it—and succeeding. "It's mainly so we won't have to come back and bother you again."

"Helen Chow. She's Chinese. Her father runs a provision company on Mott Street, or somewhere in Chinatown."

He nodded as though he were completely satisfied. Then, casually he asked for and got her number.

He looked at his subject and for a moment smiled at her, as though he knew that he was a policeman on duty, but if he had not been, he would have liked to have asked her out. He radiated understanding and masculine approval of a desirable female. "You told me," he said, "that you didn't know who killed your escort on that . . . night. I accept that. I wonder, however, if you have any ideas or thoughts of your own. You're a very intelligent young lady, and I want to hear anything you have to say."

It worked. Marcia Churchill sat silently for several seconds, then she spoke very cautiously. "I'm not sure, you understand, and when it happened I was, well, upset isn't the word."

Both policemen remained graveyard still, so as

not to break the spell.

"You see, Helen had this boyfriend who was pretty stuck on her. But he couldn't take care of her, not the way that she deserves. Of course a lot of men like her, she's exotic and very, *very* pretty. I only saw the gunman in the dark, and I only heard him speak a few words, but when he said, 'That's the last time that you'll screw anybody,' I thought for an instant, just thought, that it might be him. His name's Harold Horowitz, and he works in Wall Street."

4

When Harbizon got up in the morning it was pouring rain. The steady downpour came out of a low lead sky that sucked the energy out of his body and gave him the feeling that whatever he attempted to do that day, he was foredoomed to defeat. And whenever the rains came traffic incidents increased dramatically, as though the Boylesport drivers had never learned to cope with wet streets, as indeed they hadn't. For the most part they were people who were not used to inconvenience and who could not understand when it was thrust upon them.

The trains would run late because it would take the passengers so much longer to get on and off at each station. In New York itself cabs would be impossible, the subways would have the musty odor that wet weather always brought out, and the supposedly greatest city in the nation would virtually slow to a crawl. Decisions that were made were much more likely to be negative, and no one would say that it was good for the crops.

As he shaved, Harbizon listened to the news. There was little reported that he did not already know. The market was down almost four points on the Dow; profit taking was given as the reason.

As he drank his morning instant coffee and ate the toast he had made, he reviewed his plans for the day. Charlie Dietrich had agreed to run down the threatening letter addressed to Lockheim because the writer lived up his way. There was no question of Dietrich's ability, and if there was anything to find, he would get it. Meanwhile, Harbizon had accepted the tedious task of trying to ferret out those persons who had lost heavily during the past several months because of Lockheim. At the same time he planned to try and find out just how ethical the speculator had been in his business dealings. The fact that he had been a professional gambler—and that was the word for it—on the exchange didn't necessarily make him a scoundrel as well.

From his office he made a call in to the NYPD and talked to a lieutenant there who was working bunko and who was a specialist in stock market operations. The city man was already informed about Lockheim's death and the fact that Harbizon was working on it. He maintained good files. He suggested that they get together. Harbizon answered by promising to catch the next train.

The miserable weather continued all of the way into the city and showed no signs of a letup. Harbizon accepted it as part of a policeman's lot and made his way to the office of his colleague, hoping that there might be a cup of hot coffee waiting when he got there. It would be bad coffee, that was for sure, but it would be warm and stimulating.

The man he met was big, very wide in the shoulders, sandy-haired, and surprisingly young. Or at least he looked it. He had a reddish complexion, more than a hint of freckles, and the build of a professional wrestler. He extended a quick, cordial welcome and led the way into his small office without a shred of formality. "It's John, isn't it?" he asked.

"Right." Harbizon passed over his card.

"Ted. Nobody can pronounce Walchewski anyway. So you got yourself into a can of worms."

"It looks that way. You know the problems with a bomb case. You can't set the time that the charge was planted, the man who did it can be miles away when it goes off, and if the job is successful, there's nothing much left to work with—the evidence destroys itself."

"It was a pro job?"

"Definitely."

"Then our MO files may help out. In the meantime, you want to know about Lockheim."

Harbizon settled down and took out a fresh notebook. It was a larger one than he usually carried, and he was all set to begin on page one.

"Some coffee, John? It's not so hot, but what the hell."

Harbizon dug into his pocket for change. His host shook his head and left the office. While he was gone Harbizon studied the large bulletin board that all but covered one wall. At the top a semipermanent sign read: *No Polish Jokes*. That was the only evidence of levity. Thumbtacked below there were fifteen or twenty news stories clipped from various media. All of them reported admitted frauds, actions taken against member firms of the New York Stock Exchange, censures by the Securities and Exchange Commission, and investigations of white-collar crime. The name *Equity Funding* was prominent in some yellowing columns.

Walchewski came back with two paper cups of coffee. He planted himself behind his small desk, tossed two packets of sugar where Harbizon could reach them easily, and relaxed. "So Nat Lockheim is no more," he said almost cheerfully. "I'm sorry, of course, that his passing has given you a nasty job."

"Were you building a file on him?" Harbizon asked quickly.

"Not on Lockheim himself as much as on the whole Sphinx Wire and Cable mess. A lot of people were badly caught on that one. Some of them asked for it, but most of them were innocent investors."

"Fill me in."

Walchewski put his massive forearms on the desk. "The company itself is a sound honest outfit that turns out good products for the military. They're a prime source. About six months ago Sphinx came out with an annual report that was a sensational job. The agency that produced it made the company sound like an ideal holding."

"Exaggerated half truths, that sort of thing?"

"No, not really. All of the facts were valid as far as I know, but the tone, the bubbling optimism, was overdone in view of the general climate defense suppliers have to face right now. But to get back to the subject, with a company like Sphinx a rumor of congressional action, or a veto, can make its stock act like a Mexican jumping bean. And the traders who are just a jump ahead of these rumors, or who feed them, have practically sure bets."

"What I'm after," Harbizon said, "are some first-class suspects. People who lost heavily to Lockheim not too long ago. I just might find one who learned demolition in Nam."

"Well, John, you've got yourself a job, because stock market customers come from all over the country, and other parts of the world. And think about the brokers too. If they recommend something to their clients and then the roof falls in, where are they?"

"I thought they had big research departments to back them up."

"To some degree, but a brokerage firm gets a big position in a stock that it wants to unload. So it puts the word out to its salesmen to push it. The salesmen, or brokers, follow orders unless they want to lose their outside telephone lines. They shove the cats and dogs onto their customers like a waitress promoting last week's roasts as barbecued beef bones. They have stock in trade like everyone else, only most people don't know that."

"Was Lockheim a distinctive individual, or are there others like him?"

"Plenty, unfortunately. There are lots of traders

who use their wits and who have the privilege of buying and selling without having to pay commissions. If a stock goes up or down even a half a point they can make money, and they frequently do. If you or I go for the same stock, it will have to move a point or more before we can break even with our commissions. So the traders have a big edge."

"Getting down to specifics," Harbizon said, "I'd like to have a list, if it's at all possible, of people whom Lockheim took to the cleaners. Or Lockheim and San Marco as a team. Not the small fry in Burning Stump, Oklahoma, but here in New York and the surrounding area."

"I'll try," Walchewski promised. "I'll see what I can find out."

That was what Harbizon wanted to hear. He said the remaining necessary things and then excused himself. He was anxious to talk to the bomb specialists and to consult their MO files.

Mr. Simon R. Korngold was in a particularly vile mood. He was not a man of even temperament, and he suffered from a permanently inflated ego, so when things turned against him, as they did at times, he became unbearable—often even to himself. For almost a month he had carefully been building a heavy short position in one single stock where he knew that the earnings reports were going to be a serious disappointment. He had paid for that information and then had built up his account on the short side, some of it visibly, much of it through straw men and stock held in street name. He had what he knew to be a sure thing.

He had overlooked the fact that the president of the company had spent the four years of his college career living in the same fraternity house with a significant government official. If he had checked the sports records, he would have learned that the government man, as quarterback, had passed to the company president, as tight end, for the winning touchdown during the last eighty seconds of play in a memorable homecoming game. Mr. Korngold didn't give a damn about sports and that, in part, was his undoing.

He had never imagined that the smaller, dark-horse candidate for a major contract would be able to get the ear of the powerful man who would make the final decision. Once more the quarterback put up the ball; once more the tight end was there, this time with a sound proposition and the low bid. At a news conference the company executive released the important news. Almost immediately it hit the broad tape, and when it did the company's stock that had been depressed for months, crashed through its resistance level and soared. Korngold had been badly caught and had had to cover with heavy amounts of cash. His months of careful maneuvering had been wiped out, and he had had to swallow the biggest loss of his career as a professional trader.

He did not wait for the market to close. He could not stand to be on the floor for another minute where other traders could look at him and know that he had at last guessed wrong. He got out of the sight of those who could ridicule him and headed outside, the whole middle of his body feeling as though hot lava were running through his intestines. When he was at last in the open air he ignored the fact that it was still raining. He almost tripped as he reached the sidewalk and recovered himself awkwardly. That tiny incident inflamed him even more—it had made him look ridiculous for two or three seconds in the eyes of a few people who didn't know him and who cared even less.

It became a burning necessity to him to exert his authority; to issue commands that would be instantly obeyed because of his position—and his money. There was a lot less of it now, but he blocked that intolerable fact out of his mind. His head down against the pelting of the rain, he saw a cab coming with its top light on.

Out of the corner of his eye he saw that he had a competitor for the cab. The driver was already pulling over in response to his signal. Korngold knew well that the first passenger to hit the rear seat would win the cab and the right to use it. With total determination he leaped forward to grab the door handle and jump inside before the other man would awake to what was happening.

An odd thing happened. Another cab, that had been apparently parked, suddenly accelerated as fast as the wet pavement would allow. It struck Korngold with its right front fender hard enough to throw him off his feet and a short distance through the air before he hit the pavement. For a second or so the cab swerved as the driver fought to regain control, then it spurted forward still faster until it reached the corner. It turned against the light and disappeared into the stream of traffic that was moving northbound. Simon Korngold lay still and bleeding on the side of the street.

Because everything that happens in New York is seen by someone, and because Wall Street is a jugular of telephone lines, someone called the police. A car responded shortly and an ambulance was summoned. Simon Korngold, still living but in very critical condition, was lifted off the pavement and taken code three to the nearest available receiving hospital. There he was undressed and cared for while his wallet was searched for evidence of medical insurance that would pay the charges. When nothing was found, the business office became very upset, but it was too late to stop treatment.

Dr. Robert McKinley did his best. There was no time to assemble a team of specialists, and young Dr. McKinley therefore had to cope alone. For a resident with limited experience in the emergency ward he did phenomenally well. The case-hardened nurse who assisted him was markedly impressed. When after three quarters of an hour of intense work done on his behalf Simon Korngold breathed his last, Dr. McKinley rested his hands on the body of the man he had fought so hard to save and despite his years of training very nearly wept.

John Harbizon was patiently going through the long, involved MO lists when a young officer tapped him on the shoulder. "A call for you," he said.

Dietrich, who was on the line, was brisk. "I have the dope on Daniel Sisler, the man who wrote the letter to Lockheim."

"Any good?"

"Could be. He had demolition training in the military and he has no immediate alibi, but there's something else. About two hours ago a man was knocked down by a hit-and-run cab in front of the stock exchange. NYPD has a good and apparently very reliable witness. There are some suspicious circumstances. The car that made the hit could have been lying in wait for him."

"Does the victim fit the pattern?" Harbizon asked. He knew he would be understood.

"Yes, very closely, based on first reports. I'm going down there now. Do you want to sit in?"

"I'm on my way," Harbizon said. "When and where?"

They met in an office that was temporarily vacant. In addition to Dietrich there were two homicide men from the NYPD and the witness. The strong atmosphere of the police station did not upset the man in the least. Within seconds of meeting him Harbizon knew that he was a gem. He obviously had his head on straight, he was articulate, and he had no fear whatsoever of becoming involved. He was Mr. Ideal Citizen. His name was Henessey.

When the introductions had been made and the

door had been closed, one of the New York men took over. He was small and slender with thin hair that he wore slightly long to cover his baldness, with the result that it kept constantly falling over his forehead. He looked like an unemployed typesetter, which was strictly protective coloration. He was thoroughly experienced and competent. His partner, a younger man, was obviously new and smart enough to keep still and listen. Harbizon picked him as a comer.

"Mr. Henessey," the older man said, pushing his hair back with his right palm. "You've been very good to wait here until these gentlemen arrived. Now, if it isn't too much trouble, will you please repeat what you told us for their benefit."

"Certainly," the witness answered. "My name is Chester Henessey and I'm a printing salesman. I spend a good deal of time in the street, Wall Street that is, and in the surrounding financial area. We supply letterheads, vouchers, receipt books, and a wide line of specialized forms for the use of financial institutions." He passed across two of his business cards.

"This afternoon, at approximately two-ten, I came out of a building below the stock exchange and on the other side of the street. I had a midtown appointment at two forty-five. I had just started to walk toward the subway when I saw a cab coming with its light on. That was a break I hadn't expected, particularly on a rainy day. I signaled the driver, and he began to slow up and pull toward the curb where I was."

"Was anyone else trying to get the cab at that time?" Dietrich asked.

"No, not as far as I could see. Apparently I had been lucky. Just then I saw a man across the street slip—and for a moment I thought he was going to fall. Then, with his head down, he dashed into the street toward the cab I had just hailed."

"In other words, he was trying to beat you to it," Harbizon commented.

"Yes, I believe that's correct. It's grossly discourteous, but you know this city. I should say that I had noticed another cab pulled against the curb a little farther down the street, apparently waiting for someone. I didn't actually see that cab start up, but I caught its motion out of the side of my eye as it came up the street, accelerating rapidly despite the wet pavement. Then, without slowing at all it hit the man in the street with its right front fender. I distinctly saw him thrown through the air for a distance of about six feet."

"Can you describe that cab?" Dietrich asked.

"I'm sorry, sergeant, outside of saying that it was yellow, I can't. I was frankly shocked, and by the time I had recovered my wits, the cab had sped down the street and was much too far away for me to get the license number. I saw it go through the red light and turn into the uptown traffic stream. As far as I could tell it was a standard-sized cab and not too new, but that's all. Of course, any pursuit on foot would have been futile."

The senior New York detective nodded. "We certainly agree with that, Mr. Henessey. Tell these gentlemen the rest."

"There's very little more, actually. Someone phoned the police, obviously, since they came very fast. I went to the help of the man in the street, but I'm not medically trained and there's very little I could do."

"But you did stay until the officers came."

"Yes, of course. The ambulance came very quickly also; I was still talking with one of the officers when the man was taken away."

"What happened to your cab in the meantime?" Harbizon asked.

Henessey looked at him. "I don't know, lieutenant, I didn't think about it until this moment."

"One last question, Mr. Henessey." The homicide specialist pushed his hair back off his forehead once more. "You've given us a very lucid account of what occurred. Now, in your opinion, was it an accident, or is it possible that the victim was deliberately hit?"

Henessey considered that for a few seconds before he replied. "I would have to say that the way that the cab started up, so rapidly, and on wet pavement, certainly wasn't normal. It could have been an accident, but there is no way that the driver couldn't have known that he had hit someone. I remember now that his cab definitely swerved after the impact."

"That's important."

"Thank you, sir. I think it was either a hit and

run, or something that had been planned. But, in the latter case, considering the way that the man ran into the street, headlong and without looking, even if it was deliberate and you were able to catch the driver responsible . . ." He stopped, realizing that he was getting tangled in his sentence. "What I mean is, I'm not a lawyer, but with the given circumstances, I don't see how you could ever get a conviction."

The deli-restaurant wasn't crowded. Its worn booths had held countless forgotten customers since they had first been installed, but two of them were empty when Harbizon sat down with Dietrich to compare notes. They ordered and then relaxed. Harbizon traced a finger across the scarred Formica and banished from his mind, as best he could, the fact that his wife had left him two years before on the same date.

He was not a handsome man, he had no illusions about that. He tried to make up for it in the way he dressed and the manner in which he conducted himself. He was not yet forty, but there were lines in his face that had been etched there permanently. They were not signs of dissipation, or even of long late hours on the job. They came more from hard work and dedication. Someone had once told him that he looked like a mountaineer. When he contemplated his massive pile of work, he sometimes felt like one. He was surprised that women frequently found him attractive, and told him so.

Dietrich opened his notebook. "I've had a talk with Sisler. He readily admits having written the letter to Lockheim, but he insists that it wasn't threatening per se. Frankly, I have to agree with that. Also he signed it with his right name and gave his return address, and I can't believe he would have done that if he had contemplated any violence against him. However, it is a fact, and Sisler admits it, that he served in Nam and he has had training in demolition. He has no satisfactory alibi to cover the whole time period during which the bomb could have been planted."

"Are you satisfied that he's out of it?" Harbizon asked.

"Pretty much so. He was very straightforward. He admits that he was enraged when he lost his money through Lockheim's manipulations and he sounded off. He had a right to—it's still a free country, thank God."

"How did Sisler get onto Lockheim in the first place?"

"I've been waiting for you to ask that. He saw a column head with the name Sphinx Wire and Cable in it, so naturally he read it. The column had a lot to say about Lockheim and his heavy profits when the stock plunged. In language that stopped just short of libel, it said that he had had advance knowledge and therefore manipulated the stock to his own considerable advantage."

"Was San Marco mentioned in the article?"

"Yes, but not as prominently."

Harbizon bit into his pastrami sandwich. He chewed until he could talk easily once more, then he asked the other question that Dietrich was expecting. "Who wrote the column, Schneider and Burroughs?"

"That's right," Dietrich said.

The city of Boylesport is limited in size and in population, but it is disproportionately important as a center of both wealth and influence. It has a tax base that makes possible a level of municipal services considerably above average, the police department among them. When the Lockheim killing became a major *cause célèbre* in that carefully controlled community, the word was put out quietly, but with authority, that no expense was to be spared to bring about its resolution. The city manager had had several calls promising him all of the backing he might need, but pressing for action.

The city manager called the police chief who had been expecting to hear from him on an hourly basis for the past three days. Without any external indications of applying pressure, the city manager made his point clear and then asked some questions, all in a very restrained manner. "Who have you got on the case right now?" he asked.

"John Harbizon," the chief answered promptly. "He's very well qualified, as you know. And he's been relieved of everything else until the Lockheim killing is solved."

"Would you like some extra help?" the manager

asked. "I can request assistance from the state police and call in some private specialists in consultation."

"I certainly appreciate your support," the chief responded, "but for the moment I'm going with Harbizon. He's already working with the state police on the case, by the way. You know the salary we had to offer to get him, and he's more than proven that he's worth it. If he asks for any more backup, I'll see that he gets it. Right now our budget is in good shape."

"Then let's leave it this way. As long as the Lockheim murder remains unsolved, I'd like to suggest that you keep Harbizon on it full time and with all of the expense account he may need. I want him to follow it all of the way through. That can be done, I believe."

"Yes, it can be done, even if he might have to go into some other jurisdiction. I'll keep him on it unless it reaches the point where there is nowhere else to go. If that happens, I'll let you know."

"Fine. In the meantime, the city's official position is that we have put our top detective on it and that there isn't a better man anywhere."

"Perfectly understood," the chief said. "One suggestion. I think the city should post a reward. It will look good, and it might be helpful."

"Damn good idea," the manager retorted. "About ten thousand?"

"Right on, I'd say."

"I'll make some calls," the manager promised, and hung up.

By morning John Harbizon knew that he had carried his investigations in Boylesport as far as they would go. He had searched for additional witnesses and had all but exhausted the ones he did have. Someone had remembered seeing Lockheim's conspicuous car passing through town on its way toward its owner's estate, but that was of no practical help. An exhaustive examination of the burned-out wreck that that car had become yielded nothing new. The most tenacious questioning of every possible known person who had been on or near the railroad parking area on the fatal day got nowhere. A stakeout that had been set up just in case the bomber might decide to try again had been futile as far as the murder was concerned. A thief who was stealing electronics under the guise of a repairman was nabbed, thereby clearing up an annoying problem for several other communities up and down the railroad line.

The chief sent for Harbizon and was diplomatic. He knew that his best man could probably get a job with more prestige, and possibly more pay, almost anywhere he chose. "John," he said, "I've had a talk with the city manager and some members of the council. The upshot is that to a man they have every confidence in you and they're going to continue to have it. They understand, in short, what you're up against."

"But."

The chief shook his head. "No 'buts,' John. Just the opposite. I've been instructed to give you full

backup in any form you need. I'm to call in any help
that you want. Furthermore, the city is putting up a
ten-thousand-dollar reward for information leading
to the arrest and conviction of the bomber. Also,
until further notice you have total mobility with all
necessary expenses. They want the Lockheim
killer."

Harbizon uttered a very soft, drawn out whistle.
"Evidently they don't know who might be next."

"That's part of it, certainly. Lockheim was popular to a degree, but I suspect that it was his money
that was the attraction."

"Did you know him?"

"Slightly. Within this office, I didn't care for him,
and he indirectly cost one member of this department a lot of money he couldn't afford to lose. And
his wife is an obscenity. She got abusive with a delivery boy about six months ago and had to pay him off
to avoid a lawsuit. The kid told me that he had never
heard language like that in his life, and he wasn't
tenderly reared. But Lockheim was totaled out here,
and his killer must be brought to justice."

"I'll do my best," Harbizon promised.

As soon as he could get away, he took the train
into the city. As he rode he thought, and cemented in
his mind the idea that the killing of William San
Marco, or Moshe Feldman, was closely related and
offered a more fertile field of investigation. Also
there was his Chinese ex-mistress to be followed up,
and her boyfriend. He was relieved to know that he
had been given an almost totally free rein. It could

easily have gone the other way if the community had insisted on a sacrifice.

When he got off the train, he was slightly astonished to be met by Sergeant Charles Dietrich. "Let me guess," he said, "you called me at my office and they told you I was on my way into the city, probably on this train."

"This is the second one I've met," Dietrich admitted. "We have a break. Believe it or not, the NYPD has nabbed the cab that killed Korngold. It may be related. Korngold was a floor trader and speculator noted for his temper and his ruthlessness."

As they walked together toward the street Harbizon asked the question he wished he could ignore, and to which he already knew the answer. "Was he Jewish?" he asked.

"Yes, definitely. I checked to make sure. The first readout is that he was a very hard case who would rather bite your head off than talk to you. A minor record when he was younger, principally an assault charge. He couldn't buy out of it; the victim was a police officer."

"New York born?"

"No—Europe. Russian extraction. He was apparently born somewhere in Eastern Europe. Came here with his family when he was fifteen. He was seventeen when he tackled the cop."

Dietrich stopped for a moment and took a newspaper from under his arm. "Read," he said, and pointed to a good-sized display ad:

REWARD

$10,000

WILL BE PAID FOR INFORMATION LEADING TO THE
ARREST AND CONVICTION OF THE PERSON OR PER-
SONS RESPONSIBLE FOR THE VIOLENT DEATHS OF
OUR VALUED AND ESTEEMED MEMBERS:

NATHAN LOCKHEIM
WILLIAM SAN MARCO
SIMON R. KORNGOLD

(IN THE CASE OF MR. KORNGOLD, THE REWARD WILL
BE PAID AS SPECIFIED IF IT IS ESTABLISHED THAT HIS
DEATH WAS DELIBERATELY CAUSED. IF THE PROPER
AUTHORITIES DETERMINE THAT HIS DEATH WAS AC-
CIDENTAL, $500 WILL BE PAID FOR INFORMATION
LEADING TO THE ARREST AND CONVICTION OF THE
DRIVER OF THE CAR RESPONSIBLE FOR HIS FATAL
INJURIES.)

"That's interesting," Harbizon said when he had
read the announcement. "But even in an ad they had
to slip in the small print."

"What the big print giveth the small print taketh
away," Dietrich said. "But it's immaterial because
the police have the driver already, I think, unaided.
Now, maybe we'll get somewhere in this damn
case!"

5

Miss Helen Chow was not at all what Harbizon had expected her to be. He had somehow visualized a tiny, slim girl with wide almond eyes who would look all innocence and who underneath would be a hard, calculating little bitch. Instead he found himself confronted by a young woman who wore her black hair in a soft swirl around her face which was open, friendly, and altogether lovely. The dress she wore was informal, but in good taste. Her Chinese descent was evident in her features, but it was secondary. Within seconds Harbizon knew that she was highly intelligent and that if he didn't watch himself she would have him captivated.

Her voice was like water running under snow. "Lieutenant Harbizon? Please come in. I'm Helen Chow."

He walked into the room, following her. She gestured toward a settee, and when he had sat down she placed herself more or less beside him. He could detect her perfume then and the man inside the policeman hammered to be let out.

"What may I offer you?" she asked. "Hard, soft, hot, or cold?"

"Soft and cold." There was no drinking while on duty in Boylesport, and he automatically refused to take advantage of his position. He was alone for a minute or two, then Helen came back with two tall glasses filled with ice and some red-colored liquid. "This is a special fruit punch," she said. "See if you like it."

Harbizon took a careful swallow. "It's marvelous," he said.

He received a smile in return that would have made the Trojan horse stand up and rear. He found it a strain to believe that this appealing girl had been William San Marco's mistress. But the fact was definite, according to the information he had received. For one bitter moment he wished that policemen were compensated in the same manner as Wall Street speculators.

Helen folded one leg under her body as she turned sideways to face him. "I assume you want to talk about Bill San Marco."

"Yes, if you don't mind."

"I'd rather not, obviously, but I realize that a murder investigation takes precedence over my personal feelings. So go ahead, lieutenant, and I'll be as helpful as I can."

Harbizon began to recover his form. "That's very kind of you, Miss Chow, and in return let me assure you that I will protect your privacy as much as I'm able. I'm not here to collect gossip."

"My name is Helen, lieutenant, and I think you must be a very fine policeman."

"Why?"

"Because you're obviously a gentleman, you're conscientious, and the way you put that indicates to me that you're probably an excellent psychologist."

"Are you a psychologist, Helen?"

"No, I'm a fashion designer—in furniture and decorative fabrics."

"I suspect that pays quite well."

"It does, lieutenant, up to a point. But I'm not implying by that that I've found it necessary to augment my income in other ways. Much older ways."

Harbizon saw the trap and sidestepped neatly. "Tell me about Mr. San Marco," he invited. "Whatever you'd care to say."

She drank some of her punch and set the glass down with care. Harbizon noticed it and deduced something of her mental processes from that simple clue. "Bill San Marco was a leech," she began. "Not only in his business dealings, but in the way he managed his life. He had a gigantic ego, and the principal reason he went after money was as a means to gratify it. He was a notorious woman chaser, less for biological than statistical reasons. He saw himself as a perpetually young, dashing, romantic lover that no female could resist. Actually, he never fit that description, I'm sure, at any time in his life."

"Was he a religious man?"

"I doubt if he ever went near a temple, at least for the last thirty years. I know for a fact that he didn't

observe the high holy days, because the point arose
during the time I was living with him."

That was a deliberate lead-in that she had given
him and Harbizon knew it instantly. "Since you
know the first question I'm going to ask, suppose
you answer it," he invited.

Helen lit a cigarette and let the smoke drift silently upward. When she put it between her lips her
mouth curved into a shape that was for a bare moment totally tantalizing. Then she blew the smoke
out as if to say that what was visible was unobtain-
able. "I met San Marco at a party where, as usual,
he was trying to cut a swath wider than anyone else.
His trick was to play up to me, to show how he could
captivate the exotic flower who was present in a
black dress. What he did not know, and never
learned, was that I had gone there specifically to
meet him."

She paused, but Harbizon was far too experienced to interrupt her with a comment.

"You see," she continued, without any visible
emotion, "he had once badly cheated someone in our
community. You may have heard that we tend to
have very strong family ties."

"I know it for a fact," Harbizon said.

"Quite simply, I decided to deal with the matter.
Roger Han, a stockbroker friend of mine, made the
necessary arrangements. He knew about San Marco
and had met him once or twice. At that time I
was twenty-nine years old, still unmarried because
I hadn't found the man I wanted, and I was

not a virgin. Does that statement disturb you?"

"Not at all. I find it comforting."

She looked at him. "Why?"

"Because of what I know about San Marco. I would not like to think that he received an honor he didn't deserve."

"The man who received the honor, as you put it, took it without consulting me. I was sixteen. Subsequently, of course, I occasionally made my own choices, not always successfully, I might add."

Harbizon opened his mouth to say, "Try me," but he caught it in time.

Helen took a final puff from her cigarette and then neatly put it out. Harbizon was glad, because it had spoiled the aura of her perfume.

"I let San Marco, which was a self-chosen name as I presume you already know, make the necessary advances. I dined with him twice before he asked me to occupy the apartment he maintained for his kept women. His ego demanded that I accept. I made it clear to him that I had never accepted such a proposition, which was true, and that it would take a great deal to make me look with favor on his. He told me that I was priceless and that he could afford it, a rather visible contradiction in terms. During the time that I was supported by him I allowed him limited sexual contact, and no more, until I had recovered the entire sum that he owed, with appropriate interest. And some additional for my inconvenience. Then I contrived to have him get rid of me, otherwise he might have become difficult—even annoying."

"And that was the end of it."

"Almost. A member of my family sent him a receipt for the money he had unintentionally repaid. We desired that he should know."

"Was Mr. Horowitz aware of these— arrangements?"

"Marcia probably told you that Harold is my boyfriend. We are good friends, but it doesn't go beyond that."

"Still, I'd like to talk to him."

"By all means, if you would like. For your information, Harold's family is strictly orthodox, which is to say that they will never approve of any girl who is not of similar religious background. I don't qualify, and Harold will never go against their wishes. Therefore, we keep things within bounds. We both like medieval music, so we go to The Cloisters together and some other places. However, I can tell you right now that on the evening when San Marco was shot, Harold and I were together until quite late—very late, in fact. And if you need them, I think that I can produce witnesses."

Driver Abraham Schwartz sat in the hard chair that had been provided for him, twisted his greasy cap in his hard, muscular hands, and wished to hell that the detective talking to him would stop pushing his hair back on top of his head all of the time. Every time he tried to think, the damn cop would start fussing with his hair some more and make him forget what he intended to say.

He was in a tough spot and he knew it. He was fifty-four years old, he had had no other occupation but driving a cab for the past twenty years, and the man before him could take away his "face"—the license that permitted him to drive a hack in the city of New York. Hacking made some money, of course, but Abe Schwartz had a number of sidelines closely connected with his work that were much more profitable. Dropping tourists at certain bars, keeping special trips off his route sheet; there were all kinds of angles. But he had to keep his "face" to stay in business, and if he lost it he didn't know what the hell he could do. He wasn't fitted for anything else. Outside of New York he would have perished like a water-starved cantaloupe.

The detective took a comb out of his pocket and arranged his hair formally. As he was putting the tool back in its place, part of his thin crop of hair fell over his forehead once more. It nearly drove Schwartz crazy.

"Now let's go over it again," the detective said. "Do you deny that you dropped a fare in Wall Street shortly before two yesterday afternoon?"

Schwartz felt that his only defense was to clam up, so he did.

"I don't remember. Look at my route sheet."

There was a tap on the door that in itself told the detective a great deal. He got up without hurrying and looked outside. A voice that was out of sight of the cab driver told him, "The witness is here, and ready to make the identification."

That didn't scare Schwartz. He knew too well that fares never noticed a hackie's face or remembered his number. They usually didn't give a damn.

The witness who came in was a man dressed in a business suit, with eyes behind steel-rimmed glasses that were hostile and cold. The witness surveyed Schwartz as though he were a fish on display in the aquarium and spoke in a flint-hard voice. "You've got the right man. I'm positive. I'll testify to it."

"How are you able to recognize him?"

"I saw his cab come around the corner against the red light. It forced its way into traffic and forced my car almost into a collision situation. The man had his window open despite the rain. He leaned out and made an obscene gesture to me, then he cut in front of me ruthlessly. I memorized his face and then took his license number. I followed him for two blocks while I made sure of it."

"Did you write it down?"

"I did. I have it here, the same piece of paper. I wrote it on the edge of the *Times* that I had on the seat beside me."

That was bad. Two or three times before a witness like that had caused Schwartz serious trouble. He was had, and he knew it. The only way out now was to cop out for as little as possible. If he persisted in evading questions and remaining silent, they'd have his "face" for sure.

The detective sat down calmly, brushed his hair back on top of his head, finger-combing it as he did so. Schwartz could have climbed the wall. "Now you can tell me about it," the detective said, "or we can go the whole route. You know what that means." He touched a folder. "Your record is bad already. You should have been off the street before now."

Schwartz began to sweat. By nature he was extremely stubborn, he hated cops automatically, and his usual rule of life was never to give an inch. But the detective across the table from him had him by the balls, and the harder he squeezed, the worse it was going to hurt. A sharp bite of acid hit his stomach, and he tried once more to find a way out without giving anything.

"Another witness is coming in," the detective said, almost as though no one else was in the room. "The last fare you had, the one you dropped in the street. He had an appointment and he noted the exact time."

That did it. Schwartz felt the agony in his stomach grow. His rock hard stubbornness urged him to hang on no matter what, but he knew that would lead to worse disaster. His hatred for cops flamed within him. He had never been able to get completely away from people because driving them around was his business. And suckering them for extra bucks whenever he could. He disliked everyone and trusted no one—had grown up that way. But no matter how he felt, he had to do what was best for himself. Like a prowling big cat, that was the only thought that predominated in his mind.

"All right," he said. "But if I help you out, I gotta walk out of here and nothing more in there." He

pointed a stubby, dirt grimed finger demandingly
toward the folder.

The detective was suddenly as hard-minded as he
was himself. "You get no deal of any kind. You're
caught dead to rights, and if, just if, you don't spill
wide open and all the way, we'll look into you a little
more. You'd be surprised what we can dig up when
we put our minds to it. I've got enough right now to
pull your license permanently." His voice abruptly
was like glacial ice. "You've got fifteen seconds before I throw you in the can."

The stubbornness inside of Abe Schwartz cracked
and yielded. The world was against him, as he had
always been against it, and the bile in his stomach
was boiling.

"I picked up this fare," he said, "near Lincoln
Center. He wanted to go to Wall Street. It was bad
because it was raining, and when it's raining I can
make twice as much on short hauls, but this turkey
sticks me with a long one. But I had to take him. By
the time we got there, with the rain and all, I had
about six and a half on the clock. When I pulled up,
he handed me a five and told me to wait.

"I couldn't do nothing about it, so I sat and waited. If I went off, I'd lose a buck and a half on the
clock and the tip to boot. So I sat there for ten, maybe
fifteen minutes. I had read the guy as good for it, but
there was no way I could find him in that building
and I couldn't leave my cab. And I was losing too
damn much money sitting there."

"But your meter was running."

"Of course, Goddammit, but that does me no good if this turkey blows! By the time I had waited twelve or fifteen minutes I knew I'd been had. I was a damn fool to wait for him at all. I was burning mad, and you'da been too."

If he expected sympathy or understanding, he got none whatever.

"So I said to hell with it and hauled ass away from that curb. I could get another fare in thirty seconds, but it was dead where I sat. I was mad, I admit it, I had a right to be. Then this brainless bastard jumps out into the middle of the street right in front of me. Jesus Christ couldn't have stopped in time. I knew I brushed him, but it was his damn fault, so I got the hell out of there. I took more than a six-buck loss on the meter and in that time I could have made more with a tip. It wasn't any of my business because it wasn't my fault."

He tried to look as if he believed it, and failed.

The detective got up and opened the door part way. "Take him away," he ordered.

Abe Schwartz got to his feet and cursed the world that hated him from the day of his birth. He only endured it because there was no other place to go, at least not any where he could make a buck. He felt sharper pains still in his stomach as he was led away.

John Harbizon fed two quarters into the slot of the vending machine and pulled the appropriate plunger. In response a small package dropped into the tray in the bottom; he picked it up without much hope. The so-called sweet roll on display looked as though it had been defeated before it had ever been started as dough. Across the top it had a thin brushing of what passed for glaze. Harbizon had bought it anyway out of a certain sense of desperation. He had not had any breakfast, and he wanted something that was presumably edible to go with the cup of bad coffee the next machine would provide.

While he waited for Dietrich to arrive he peeled the wrapping off the roll and took an experimental bite. He had expected very little, but the roll was worse than he had imagined. He looked at it for a moment, wondering how with all of the skills of modern science a product could be turned out that was so utterly tasteless. He would have thrown it away, but the only other available selection was a packet of four tiny cracker sandwiches with a minute amount of peanut butter for filling. He had tried it once and found it ghastly. As he made the best of the inevitable situation he wondered why something better could not be provided for the men and women whose job it was to see that the city did not cannibalize itself with crime. Take away the NYPD and in a month there wouldn't be anything left of the supposedly greatest city on earth.

Harbizon ate the miserable sweet roll and drank his acid coffee until Dietrich came in. Neither of them properly belonged in a Manhattan police station, but they were officers of the law and as such were welcomed. They might even write a letter to somebody about the food.

Dietrich was ready with a report. "I talked with Harold Horowitz, the Chinese doll's boyfriend. In essence he confirmed everything that she told you— the nature of their relationship, the religious barrier to it developing any further, and the statement that they were together on the night that San Marco was shot. He said that they could produce witnesses, but when I asked for some, he couldn't come up with anything definite. Said he would try."

"Which could mean that he wants to look for someone to lie for him."

"Exactly. At this point he's probably out of it, but I would like to see that alibi cemented down. He admitted knowing Marcia Churchill. Said he had talked to her several times, so the idea of her recognizing his voice is still a possibility. And there's motive. He's a very intense person, and no matter how he may have accepted it on the surface, he hardly liked the idea that San Marco had been laying his girlfriend. And you remember what the Churchill girl said the gunman had told San Marco, 'That's the last time you'll screw anyone.' "

Harbizon had his own notebook out. "That remark could be taken two ways, of course, as you realize. Literally, or figuratively."

"Or both, John. Literally, and figuratively in the sense that he had made his living for some time in some possibly questionable activities."

"If Horowitz can come up with a valid proof of his alibi, what's our next step?"

"I say we hit the stock exchange again and find

out all we can about the victims' associates—particularly their trading opponents. I assume they had some."

"Lockheim, probably, but I'm not so sure about San Marco. He was a specialist, remember."

"I know, and we can expect to encounter the grand cover-up if anything at all was out of line. What are your ideas?"

"We could do that together, but if you want to ferret alone, I'll see what I can get out of those columnists we met. It's their job to dig up the dirt about the market, so they have to know a lot about what's going on."

Dietrich snapped his notebook shut. "Done. I'll go down and sweat that PR man, Fellini. If he doesn't come through, I'll threaten to go upstairs to Stone, who I'm sure is his boss. Stone knows that we have a double homicide that's definite plus the Korngold thing, so he isn't going to try to be cute."

A New York detective came into the coffee room, a coin in his left hand. With his right he brushed his hair back from off his forehead. "Speaking of Korngold . . ." Harbizon said. When the New York man had his ration, Dietrich signaled to him and he joined him.

"I'm sorry," Dietrich said, "I didn't get your name last time."

"Elliott."

"What's the latest on the Korngold matter?"

"I was about to call you on that," Elliott answered. "We had a witness, another one, who came forward and ID'ed the cab that made the hit. We brought the driver in. I just finished questioning him a few minutes ago."

Harbizon and Dietrich were both listening intently.

"The driver is a hard case, known to us. His name is Abe Schwartz, and he's on file for suspected minor racketeering, running errands for the mob now and then, and clipping tourists when he isn't otherwise occupied. He feeds johns into the come-on bars and is a short-change artist. He has one MO: grab the buck."

"What's his story?" Dietrich asked.

Elliott summarized the interview, carefully including every pertinent point. It took him less than a minute.

Harbizon worked the muscles of his jaw while he thought. "What you're telling us," he said, "is that if the driver's story stands up, the killing was an accident."

"You've got it," Elliott told him. "We have him, of course, for felony hit and run, so he'll be off the street for good. But as of now I can't see murder, and what's more, it was at least partly Korngold's fault."

Harbizon remained silent, still thinking. "Let me tell you what's been bothering me," he said at last. "There are a lot of far-out organizations around—you remember the SLA, then there's the American Nazi Party, and a lot more. All three of the victims were Jewish. I've been hoping to God that it was a coincidence, because if it wasn't, we might be up against the worse thing we've ever faced."

"Exactly," Dietrich agreed.

"The apparent fact that the Korngold killing was accidental takes off some of the curse. It shortens the odds a great deal. And a man named Abe Schwartz is more likely to be Jewish than gentile."

"I thought of that, of course," Elliott said. "Terrorism is something that we have to watch out for on a continuously alert basis. I'm inclined to agree that we're dealing with a not-too-strong coincidence, because, admittedly, there is a high percentage of Jews in Wall Street. But when it looked as though there might be three in a row—well, I didn't get much sleep last night."

"Welcome to the club," Harbizon said.

From that point everything appeared to go downhill. Fellini, at the stock exchange, went through all of the motions of being helpful, but when Dietrich left him, he went out by the same door that he came in.

When Harbizon tried to make an appointment to see Schneider and Burroughs, he learned that Bert Schneider was out of town and that his partner was up to his eyeballs in work. Burroughs offered to cooperate fully and then asked that the conversation be restricted to five minutes. He wasn't putting on an act, he had a deadline to meet.

The upshot of that conference was that there was so much hanky-panky going on in the market that the case of Sphinx Wire and Cable was more representative than unique. "Read the files of the *Wall*

Street Journal and see for yourself," the columnist advised. "We have scrapbooks full of clippings of financial wrongdoing, and there's no end in sight."

"When you have a few more minutes, could we talk about it then?" Harbizon asked, his voice mild.

Gene Burroughs relented. "O.K., I guess I've been letting things get to me a little too much lately. Look at the picture this way . . . you save up some money or come into an inheritance and what do you do? You can put it in the bank or the savings and loan and get some interest. The big plus is that your funds are safe and you can count on some return. The bad part is that the rates of inflation we've had to live with for the past several years have so reduced the buying power of the dollar, that savings deposits have often shrunk in value despite the interest they earned.

"What the market professes to offer is a hedge against inflation, plus a return. The theory is simple. A hundred shares of stock in a sound company are worth so much buying power. Therefore, if the value of the dollar goes down, the price will go up. If it worked that way it would be great, but the market is fueled by literally billions of dollars. That much cash, in turn, attracts every kind of vulture and parasite who thinks that he can get a chunk of it, usually by taking it away from someone else. So the price of a stock doesn't rest simply on the value of the company it represents or even its earnings. Furthermore, speculation is encouraged by all kinds of tricks and devices—option sales, trading against the box, you name it. The pros set it up, and they usually have a continuing field day, especially if they don't have to pay commissions."

"You know my present assignment," Harbizon said. "I need some help. I'm not an expert in the stock market. You are. Narrowing it down to Sphinx Wire and Cable, who else was involved? Did Lockheim have a trading rival, somebody he beat out? Were any of the Sphinx executives themselves hit hard? I know that company officers often have sizable stock holdings in their own firms. Is there anyone else at all in the picture whom you might know about?"

Burroughs thought hard. Harbizon knew that he didn't want to answer that question, not when it contained within it the built-in suspicion of murder. Finally, when the answer came, it was with considerable reservation. "I want to do all that I can for you, but I don't want to be sued. So please, treat this as confidential. What I mean is, don't give me, or Bert and me, as the source."

"Depend on it," Harbizon said.

"All right. There's a man named Cecil Forrester. He's a respected stockbroker who for years handled some very large accounts. His track record was one of the best. Then somehow he was cornered by this Sphinx Wire and Cable thing. You see, it's basically a very good company, soundly financed, and with an excellent product line. The kind of thing you or I might buy for ourselves. I can't give you the details offhand, but Forrester was very badly hurt. His clients suffered and naturally they blamed him. He made a considerable stink and seriously talked about filing a complaint with the SEC. He's just heavy enough that he might make it stick and put some very important people squarely on the spot. There was even talk that he might force a congressional investigation of the whole securities business. If that were to happen right now, the pavement would be littered by window jumpers who wouldn't be able to escape the heat."

"This must be common knowledge, then," Harbizon noted.

"It is. Everyone in the street knows it. But they don't know Forrester. He has an interesting background. Before he took up his present occupation he was, according to a limited rumor, a James Bond type. At least I'm pretty sure that he worked for some years for British Intelligence."

6

During the three months that he had been head of the Beverly Hills office of Williams, Sloan, Furman & Brown, Ben Sorenson had already cut a wide swath. As soon as he had been promoted to his new job he had been made a vice-president, a title that was highly impressive lettered on the glass paneling that enclosed his comfortable office. The customers who read it were not always aware that the big stock exchange member firm had a multiplicity of vice-presidents and that the title as it stood had largely come to mean head salesman.

Ben sat with a full view of the many cubicles in which his sales staff was housed, like so many bees in a hive. On the far wall a long, narrow electronic board kept up a continuously traveling display of quotations that reflected the activity on the trading floor of the New York Stock Exchange. Underneath it a somewhat smaller panel reported the transactions on the American Stock Exchange. Lastly, a projection device supplied a readout of the broad tape: the more-or-less continuous news wire that supplied business news likely to affect stock prices.

To one side a number of chairs had been placed to accommodate the tape watchers, some of whom sat there by the hour trading what was left of their eyesight for the continuous stream of financial information. Sometimes, when he was sure he was speaking to someone who would sympathize with his viewpoint, Ben liked to refer to that section of the office as the Home for Elderly Hebrews.

At thirty-four Ben was already successful, and in his own opinion he deserved every bit of it. He was indisputably handsome, an asset that had been of incalculable value in forming new romantic attachments. He stood an even six feet, wore expensive clothes, and had cultivated the habit of speaking in a way that won the confidence of men and the admiration of women. He felt that he could hardly ask for more than that. He had a very good income from his own commissions, his override, bonuses when they came, and those transactions he made on his own account when he was equipped with some special information. Nature and circumstance had both been very good to Ben Sorenson, and he had neglected no opportunity to translate his existing assets into hard cash or other things that he wanted. To have done less would have been to ignore the endowments he had been given.

Jack Rampole, an unspectacular but steady salesman, paused at the doorway and when he received a nod came in. "We've got another idiot letter, this time from Mrs. Betty Williamson. Remember her?"

"Vaguely."

"She came in off the street ten or eleven months ago—before you joined us. She had some securities left to her by a brother. She wanted us to handle the account."

"I remember now," Ben said. "She gave us full discretionary powers, didn't she?"

"In writing. Of course she said all of the usual things—she wanted dividends, stocks that would be sure to hold their value with a chance for growth, and personal attention to her account. For her first trades I put her into a hundred of Bethlehem and another hundred of Kodak. When she was happy with that I gave her a thousand of Pacific Oil Exploration. You know we were to unload that."

"A thousand was a little much, five hundred would have been better. Did you call her first?"

"Yes, she told me whatever I thought was right for her she would approve. So I made it a point to put her into an electronics outfit where she gained three points. That made her very happy. But now she's written threatening to write to the president of the company about the Pacific Oil."

"What did she buy it at?"

"Nineteen and five eighths."

Sorenson punched a machine on his desk. "It's back up to four and three eighths," he said. "Call her and tell her to hang in there—that we expect the stock to recover any day."

"I've already done that."

Ben leaned forward. "All right, give me her number. I'll call her myself and tell her that I'm taking over her account personally; that ought to shut her up for a while. And do me a favor. Call Marisconi's and have them reserve a table for me at one fifteen. Today is Thursday and that's the abalone special."

"Right away," Rampole responded. For a moment he wondered if he were going to be issued an invitation, then he knew better. It would be that girl from the university, of course.

At three o'clock Ben made a show of returning to his office. He made the call to the Williamson woman and confidently assured her that he would give her account his complete personal attention. He listened with amusement, carefully concealed, as she again recited her complaint and then warmly thanked him for his personal interest. "I do so need help," she said. "You see, soon my investments are going to have to be what I will be living on."

He made a note on his pad to put her into something where she would make two or three hundred dollars. He could usually find a way to do it, and it would shut her up for a long while. After that she'd have to take her chances like everyone else. The name of the game was commissions and that was his catechism.

Most of the office being empty, he called Wanderlust, Inc., and spoke directly with the president of the small house trailer manufacturer. Although they had never met, the executive was quite open and honest with him. "Yes," he said, "our backlog is up a little and now that the fuel shortage fears are over, at least for the time being, it's getting easier to sell our products. We do make very good units and our prices are competitive."

"I assumed that, sir." Ben was all polished smoothness on the line. "And I know your stock is available over the counter . . ."

"Yes, but in very limited supply. This is largely a family-held business, although we did officially go public three years ago. Three or four transactions could affect the price noticeably, so please bear that in mind."

"I certainly will," Sorenson declared, truthfully. "I want to come down and see your plant one of these days."

"Do that, sir, we're not too far. And if you see one of our models that you like, perhaps we may be able to do something for you."

"That's most enticing. Thank you very much."

As soon as he had hung up he called his contact at the Pacific Stock Exchange and directed him to buy three thousand Wanderlust, Inc., for his own account, on margin.

That was enough work for the afternoon. In the morning he would call about fifteen people whom he knew would buy anything that he recommended and tell them that Wanderlust was going to report new high earnings and that he had advance information of the data. If that resulted in ten or eleven buys of Wanderlust, and that was practically a certainty, it should push the price up two and a half to three points—perhaps even more. The rise, in turn would trigger more orders which he would fill from his own holding. If he played it right he should be able to clear several thousand on the deal. And the stock might stay up there awhile, which would give some of his pigeons a chance to make a buck also, that is, if they had the sense to sell. If they didn't, then they would ride it right down again, but they would have no squawk coming because he had told them that it was going to go up and it had. Of course, not all of them could get out, because the sell orders would drive the price down once more.

He got into his Porsche and drove to the house in the canyon. Dorothy wouldn't be there for some time, but it didn't matter. It was a common enough name, but it was attached to an uncommon girl. She had money in her own right and the small canyon house that featured a spectacular view. She was a spectacular view herself when she walked around casually naked in the living room, as she often did for his entertainment. Despite the fact that he had been living with her for almost a year, he had not yet tired of the sight of her body. Perhaps because she was also the most sensational woman that he had ever taken to bed.

As he let himself into the house, the damned dog that she insisted on keeping came running up to offer him wet and unwanted affection. Sorenson hated the animal. It had once jumped onto the bed just at the moment when he was reaching one of the greatest climaxes of his life, and had licked one of his bare buttocks. The dog had to go. But Ben knew that Dorothy was aware of his dislike for it, and he did not dare kill it until the time would be right. Then he would pitch its body over into the bottom of the canyon where it would lie undisturbed for weeks, even months. No one ever went down there. It was too overgrown and thorny to encourage exploration.

He made himself a drink and sat down with a sense of easy freedom. He liked the house very much, and it afforded exactly the kind of privacy he valued so much. None of his clients would ever be able to find him there, and his office had strict instructions to call him only in the event of a real emergency.

As if to match his thoughts, the phone rang. Since the number was in the most restricted category, he answered with a plain, "Hello."

Dorothy's voice came over the wire. "Lover, I'm roped into that damn thing in San Diego. I've got to leave in a few minutes and I won't be back until tomorrow afternoon. Can you make out O.K.?"

Damn right he could make out, but he had to check something first. "How about clothes and things?" he asked. "You'll be coming for those, won't you?"

"No, I packed a bag and brought it with me this morning—just in case. I'm sorry."

Ben Sorenson left her with the feeling that life would end for him until she returned, then he hung up. When the dog came and put his forepaws in his lap, trying again for a return of affection, the wild idea hit him that right then would be a good time to strangle the damn mutt, but then his salesman's sense told him that it would be wrong. The way to do it would be to leave his office sometime during the hours when he would usually be there, and then get rid of it. Then he would arrange to be delayed until after Dorothy had come home. She would be all upset because the dog would be missing and he would help her search. It was ideal because he had to leave before six every morning in order to be in his office at seven when the market opened in New York.

He shut the dog in a back room and then picked up the phone once more. When the answer came he said, "Marion?"

"Yes?"

"Ben. You remember the little business matter I've been trying to arrange?"

"Yes."

"The contract has just been signed. I'll see the other party again late tomorrow."

"I see. Perhaps we should celebrate."

"I'm all for it. Can your husband join us?"

"No, I'm sorry. Phil is out of town again—somewhere in the Midwest. I don't expect him back until Sunday night."

It was perfect. She was willing, her husband was out of the way, Dorothy was gone, and there was nothing whatever to interfere. "Come anytime," he said. "We have lots to talk about."

Marion breathed something over the line that he ignored. When a fish was hooked, it was hooked and that was all that mattered.

When she arrived he showed her in with proper formality just in case anyone was looking. That was all but impossible since the canyon house was quite isolated, but he never took any unnecessary chances. Once the door had been closed he went into his "I couldn't wait another moment" routine which, this time, was close to the truth. He had dreamed of having her ever since he had met her and Phil at a party somewhere in Malibu. Every time that he had watched her walking across the floor he had had an insatiable desire to have her despite her six-foot-three, two-hundred-and-twenty-pound husband who had once played professionally at middle line backer.

She would be number one hundred, and he could not think of anyone he wanted more. Even the fading Hollywood actress he had had three weeks before for all her fame wasn't quite up to it. Marion was.

He made some drinks and then spent the next fifteen minutes showing her how totally considerate and charming he could be. He turned on his most winning smile, the same one that had sold ten thousand shares of Pacific Exploration to a normally sharp-witted attorney, and ignored the whinings of the dog that was pleading to be let out.

Then Marion looked at him with a face that he hadn't been able to erase from his mind. "I want to tell you something," she said. "This is the first time. I've never cheated on my husband before."

He knew better than to say anything in response

to that. Instead, he sat down very close to her and sent out vibrations to tell her that this hallowed moment meant at least as much, if not more, to him. He put his arm around her and kept the thought in his mind that they were true mates. If she had anything in her at all, she would read it and respond.

It took him almost an hour to get her out of her clothes. She protested a little so he became masterful as he knew she wanted. When he had the last stitch off her he looked at her body with genuine hunger. Within two minutes he had her on the bed and he had begun his standard program of caressing her body. She responded to it magnificently. Almost at once she was eager for him so that every second of delay was an agony. He mounted her smoothly and she sighed deeply. "One hundred!" he said silently to himself.

He wanted her to stay the night, but she was too afraid that her neighbor would notice she had not come home. If that happened, the neighbor would be certain to mention it to Phil sometime when he was out in the yard. It was too much risk. They had two more drinks, an hour's rest, and then more sex. After that they dressed and because he had decided that return engagements would be well worth the arranging, he took her to dinner at a restaurant noted for its privacy and intimate atmosphere. She saw no one she knew, but just in case, they agreed that he had been advising her on some possible stock investments.

He went back to the house in the canyon enormously well satisfied with himself. He knew for a certainty that Wanderlust, Inc., would have to go up during the next two days, and he already knew how he was going to hide his profit from the Internal Revenue Service. He went to bed alone; he would have preferred otherwise, but while he refused to accept even the vaguest suggestion that the years were beginning to erode his vitality, he was content not to test his powers any further. Besides, he needed the rest.

He was deeply asleep when an inconspicuous car parked a quarter of a mile away down the canyon road. People often did that sort of thing at odd hours, and most of the canyon residents paid little attention. The man who got out had a bag with him, but at that hour everyone who might have noticed was sound asleep. Even if a police patrol had come past, there was nothing to attract attention. It hardly mattered because within seconds the man with the bag disappeared over the rim of the road and was out of sight, somewhere in the tall growth of the canyon.

With the assurance of someone who knows precisely what he is doing, he made his invisible way through the scattered brush until he was just below the house where Ben Sorenson lay asleep, wild and undisciplined erotic dreams running through his head. A wide smile curved his lips as he turned over and took a fresh position between the satin sheets.

The man with the bag surveyed the ground and then set about his work with neat, careful precision. When he was sure that everything was under control, he climbed up thirty more steps until he was under the house itself. That was easy, because it was semicantilevered over the canyon rim. The ground was totally dry and his deliberately wrong-sized shoes left the faintest of impressions on its parched surface.

From the bag that he carried he took out a small arsenal of electrician's tools and two short lengths of substantial insulated wire which were equipped with alligator clips at both ends. It did not take him long to tap a section of flexible conduit. With pliers he peeled away a small part of the spiral casing and after separating the wires it contained, he fixed one of the clamps onto each one. Since the two short lengths of wire he had brought were then energized, he kept them well apart. He was twenty minutes early, but he was completely out of sight, and the chance of anyone taking an interest in the car he had parked was almost nil. If a police unit were to run the number, the readback would report that it was rented and that everything was in order.

Because the flooring above him was not insulated, he clearly heard the alarm clock ring in the master bedroom even though it was well to his right. After a half minute he heard the sound of footsteps across the floor. Mr. Benjamin Sorenson, who would sell anything to anyone for a commission, had wakened for the day.

Sorenson went into the bathroom which, not by accident, was directly above the place where the man underneath had done his work. With controlled pa-

tience the unseen man waited until he heard the
toilet flush, then the intermittent running water as
Sorenson shaved. He checked his watch and discovered that the time was within four minutes of what
he had anticipated. His man still had to brush his
teeth which would take a minute and a half. When
that time was up, Sorenson entered the shower.
Within a few seconds there was a rush of water and
the drain pipe under the house began to give off
sounds.

With neat care the man attached one of the alligator clamps to a drain lug, securing a good ground.
Then he put on an insulating glove, took a careful
grip on the other lead, and listened for a few seconds
more. The sounds that came to him were partially
distorted by the steady flow of water, but apparently
the man in the shower was singing. It would have
been appropriate if it had been a penitential hymn,
but the man underneath the house very much doubted that it was. Then he opened the other clip and let
it close over the hot water pipe.

The singing was instantly interrupted by a sudden mounting shriek which was cut off in mid-
flight. Three seconds later there was a muffled thud
against the flooring above.

The man under the house let the current flow for
a few more seconds, then he disconnected his kit.
With the pliers he carefully rewrapped the spiral
covering of the flexible conduit; when he had finished the repair was so neat it was all but invisible.
He put all of his tools back into the bag together with

the wire leads and the insulated glove. Then, his work done, he went back down the pathway he had chosen, brushing away his tracks behind him. Hardly ten minutes later he drove quietly away in his rented car. It was just six, and in that moneyed area there was not another soul awake to take note of his presence.

The body was not discovered until that evening. The first indication was a series of female screams loud enough to be heard elsewhere in the canyon. That upset someone enough to call the cops. An LAPD black-and-white cruiser responded with officers Jerry Abarian and Frank Toth aboard. After ringing the bell several times they were admitted by a young woman who was holding a tall, half-filled glass in her shaking left hand. "I just came home and found him there," she burst out without preliminary. "I didn't touch anything—I couldn't."

Officer Abarian went in the direction she was pointing. He was the senior man and much more experienced in the sight of sudden death than was his younger partner. He found the body quickly. The water was still running, but there was less of it on the floor than he expected. He noted that when the nude man in the shower stall had collapsed, he had done so in a way that had not forced the door open. Consequently, the water had gone steadily down the drain, which, also by chance, had been left clear.

A first quick examination of the circumstances

indicated that it had been an accidental death, but Abarian noted that the deceased was a quite young man, well muscled, and not a very likely heart attack victim. Since the now cold water had been running on the body for an unknown period of time, the usual tests for body heat would be out the window. He phoned in and reported the circumstances.

Homicide investigators Marlow and Hatch were part of the second response. While Officer Abarian sat in a chair carefully printing his report in block letters, Marlow talked in a soothing manner with the young woman who had discovered the body and calmed her down as much as he could. He was an expert at that sort of thing, and presently she was anxious to supply him with all of the details she knew.

"His name was Ben Sorenson," she began. "We've been living together here for about ten months. He is—was—a stockbroker, a vice-president and head of the Beverly Hills office of his firm."

"A stockbroker, you say?"

"Yes. He must have been a very good one because he made scads of money. He was very, very smart, and he was always talking about some deal that he was putting over. Don't ask me about them—I only pretended to listen when he described them, but they were always complicated. I was away yesterday, in San Diego, and I only got back a little while ago."

"Just when was that, Miss Abrams?"

"Within the hour. My God, I wasn't watching

the time! I'd better take a Valium." She got to her feet, took three steps, and then stopped. "They're in the bathroom," she said.

Marlow went and got the small bottle for her. She gulped two of the tiny pills and then washed them down with her highball.

"When did Mr. Sorenson usually get up in the morning?" he asked.

"Before six. You see, he had to be in his office by seven, because that's when the market opens in New York. When people call him at the opening, they expect him to be there."

"The last time you saw him, was he in good health?"

"Oh yes, he's the healthiest man I know."

"Did he ever complain to you about dizziness or pains in the chest?"

"No, never."

"Do you know the name of his doctor?"

"We never discussed that."

"What about his next of kin? Was he married?"

"He was, but he isn't now. He has some family back in Minnesota, but I don't know anything about them."

"Did he get his personal mail here or at the office?"

"Everything went to the office. No mail for him came here at all."

Hatch came back into the room. He nodded to his partner and then spoke in a matter of fact voice that was easy on the nerves. "The medical examiner will be here shortly. He won't be long and then the body can be removed." He looked at the young woman who was again resorting to her drink. "Excuse me," he asked, "but have you had any girlfriends staying with you recently?"

Dorothy gave him a quick, penetrating look charged with suspicion. "What did you find?" she asked.

Hatch moved a hand in a casual horizontal gesture. "Nothing, really. I was just wondering."

"You found something. I know it. This is my house. I own it, and I'm entitled to know."

Marlow knew that her continuing cooperation was essential and that there was no way that anything could alienate her from her boyfriend any more. "Tell her," he advised. He had a pretty good idea what the evidence might be.

"Just some long blond hairs in the drain," Hatch said. "They're new."

Dorothy swallowed hard and, despite herself, she raised her hand to touch her own naturally chest-nut-colored hair.

7

John Harbizon sat quietly in the outer office under the eye of a secretary-receptionist who had obviously been chosen, at least in part, for eye appeal. By her accent she was British, and the way that she quietly sat at her desk suggested that she was experienced in her job.

The room itself was wood paneled, probably with synthetically coated plywood, and decorated with a dignified reserve. There were no plastic plants gathering dust in corners where no living thing of its supposed kind could possibly grow and no forced effort to carry out a "theme." The chair in which Harbizon was sitting was comfortable; it had been designed by someone who was more interested in its function than appearance. Harbizon chalked the whole room up as a point in favor of the man he was waiting to meet. The more ostentatious types usually had decor smeared on by a heavy hand with nothing else allowed to intrude.

A light glowed on the telephone and the receptionist rose. "Mr. Forrester is free now," she said. "I'm very sorry you were kept waiting."

"That's quite all right," Harbizon responded, then he walked toward the door that she was courteously holding open for him.

Cecil Forrester rose from behind his desk to greet his guest. He was quietly and neatly dressed. As he stood up Harbizon decided that he was carrying perhaps ten pounds more than he should, but it was well distributed. He might have been fifty, and when he shook hands Harbizon had a definite feeling that he was exceptionally fit for his age. The secretary closed the door and they were alone.

Harbizon passed over his card. Forrester took it and then asked if he might see some credentials. As Harbizon produced his laminated ID he decided that the man before him might very well have been with British Intelligence; most people would have accepted his card as proof of identity which, of course, it was not.

Forrester indicated a chair. "Sit down, lieutenant," he said, "and tell me what I can do for you."

"I understand, Mr. Forrester, that you are a stockbroker."

"Financial adviser, lieutenant, which is quite a different thing. I do make transactions on behalf of my clients, but I go through a member firm of the New York Stock Exchange when I do." His accent was definite and presumably British, but to Harbizon's untutored ear it could also have been either Australian or South African. He had been fooled on that point before.

"But you are fully familiar with the securities

market," Harbizon suggested.

"Yes, that's true, but I am naturally stronger in some areas. What do you have in mind?"

"Mr. Forrester, I am investigating the recent death of Nathan Lockheim. By any chance, did you know him?"

"No, I did not." The answer was prompt, but carefully given.

"Are you aware how he died?"

"According to the news reports, he was blown up in his car."

"That's correct. Not long afterward another man, William San Marco, also died violently under unusual circumstances."

"If you are implying a question, I didn't know him either."

"Did you know *of* either of these men?"

Forrester nodded, his composure unruffled. "Yes, I knew of them."

At that point Harbizon deliberately shifted his tack. "Mr. Forrester, I know very little about the stock market, but I do know that both of those men were involved with the same stock."

It was clearly a baited question, but Forrester answered it anyway. "You mean Sphinx Wire and Cable. San Marco was the floor specialist; Lockheim was a heavy trader in the stock."

"A speculator, in other words."

"Yes."

"Now . . ." Harbizon leaned forward just a little. "I'm conducting a murder investigation, so some of the niceties have to go by the board. Not for quotation, what was Lockheim's reputation?"

"About the same as a cobra at a Sunday school picnic," Forrester answered without turning a hair.

"Did he manipulate the stock?"

"Yes, of course he did. Technically everyone manipulates whenever they buy or sell any security, but that's beside the point."

"How did he manage it?"

"By means of capital." Forrester broke his formal tone for a moment. "I take it that you want a candid answer that I won't be liable for later."

"Yes, both ways."

"Very well. Nat Lockheim had some money of his own, but not enough for large-scale speculating until he married a woman who had all the money he could possibly need. After that, he became an almost sure winner."

"Why?" Harbizon asked.

Forrester turned in his chair a little, preparing himself to answer that. "I ran into a man once on a train who offered to match pennies with anyone interested. You know how that works. You stack up whatever pennies you have, he does the same, then you compare piles. If the two top pennies match, you take them; if they don't, he does. And so on down through the pile. Before long he had won all of the pennies of everyone who had played with him."

Harbizon thought. "But if the game was honest, the odds were exactly even."

"That's right, lieutenant, but it's also very deceptive, because the man who started the game couldn't lose except by a miracle. Look at it this way. You are going to fight an enemy who has one hundred soldiers, all equally brave and skillful. You have an army of only ten men."

"But that isn't the same thing."

"Oh yes it is. Your ten men engage ten of the enemy; the other ninety enemy troops are held in reserve. According to the law of averages, if they fight until every man is wounded or captured, what will the outcome be?"

"I will lose five men, and the enemy will lose five."

"Exactly, but you have now lost 50 per cent of your total resources; your enemy has lost only 5 per cent. Even if your army wins six to four, or even seven to three, you still lose because the enemy only takes a 7 per cent loss while you sustain 30 per cent. The man on the train won constantly because he had two or three hundred pennies. No one else had anything like that number."

Harbizon digested that, and saw the logic behind it. "What you are saying is, a man with ten thousand dollars can't defeat a man with a hundred thousand."

"That's it—barring a miracle."

Harbizon shot a quick question. "Was Lockheim in cahoots with San Marco?"

Forrester laughed, and gained a little time. "An unusual word, lieutenant, but I know what it means. I would say that it was likely. Off the record, of course. I won't say so in court."

Harbizon declined to discuss that. "Can you see revenge as a motive for the killing of those two men?"

"That's in your field of specialty, lieutenant, not mine. But clearly, it's a possibility. You can also take it a step further and consider whether or not someone might have wanted simply to clean up the scene—keep the weasels out of the chicken coop."

Harbizon had thought of that, and often. He tried another shot. "I heard, strictly unofficially, that you were once in a field close to law enforcement."

Forrester appeared to ignore that. "I presume that you've heard about the incident in California last night."

"What incident?"

"It's probably totally unrelated, but a stockbroker with not too good a reputation died very suddenly under suspicious circumstances."

"Where in California?"

"Los Angeles. Of course, that's a long ways away."

"It takes less than six hours to fly to Los Angeles," Harbizon snapped. "And there are a number of planes every day."

That new information so absorbed Harbizon's attention, he left unaware that his carefully timed key question had been left unanswered.

When he called his office, there was a message to phone Sergeant Dietrich. He presumed that it would be about the California thing and was a little embarrassed that he hadn't heard of it sooner. He got Dietrich on the line and waited.

"John," the detective began. "I've been at work checking out some of the people in this case. Right now, about the only one who couldn't have shot San Marco is Marcia Churchill who was otherwise engaged at the time."

"It's still a possibility," Harbizon warned.

"I realize that, and she did have the opportunity to get rid of the gun. She told a story very embarrassing to herself, but it could have been a pretty cute piece of misdirection."

Harbizon immediately felt better. "I believe that part of it, because the medical examiner confirmed that the deceased had had very recent sexual intercourse."

"Granted, but suppose while he was getting his breath back, she shot him. She got out of the back seat first and *pow*. It all fits."

The trouble was, it did.

"What do you know about this California thing?"

"Not much. I've talked with LAPD and they don't have very much so far. The victim, if he was one, was in his early thirties, in apparently excellent physical condition. He dropped dead in the shower and was found there."

"After exercise? Tennis, something like that?"

"Negative. Apparently he was taking his morning shower when he keeled over. He was expected at his office by seven and he didn't show. He was almost always there, because that was where he made his money."

"Same type of guy?"

"Same type of guy, a wheeler-dealer in the market. But there's one big difference."

"Yes?"

"His name was Sorenson. That checked out as his real name, so thank the Lord, he probably wasn't Jewish."

Harbizon hesitated before he went on. "What else have you got?"

"Daniel Sisler, the letter writer who told Lockheim he would be better off dead, has been moonlighting a little. Using his skills as an explosives expert. He has had access to some quite interesting material."

"Alibi?"

"Nothing checkable. He states where he was, but it can't be proven. Do you remember Harold Horowitz?"

"Yes."

"Then you remember that he and his Chinese girlfriend alibied each other. I believe they said they could produce witnesses. I invited him to do that, just to keep things tidy."

"And he couldn't."

"That's right—he couldn't. And the more I talked with him, the more uncomfortable he became."

"A tag might be a good idea."

"He's got one on him now. At the moment, I'm very interested in that young man. And in his lady friend. I gather she has plenty of nerve."

Harbizon could have said something about that, but he didn't.

Detective Marlow, who was assigned to homicide investigation by the LAPD, was named Emil. That was the way that he was listed in the official records of the department, but none of his associates could recall any time when that name had been used. From the day that he had signed on and had been sent to the academy, he had been tagged with the name Philip. He rather liked it, and during his twelve years as a policeman there had been three or four instances of his being taken for that fictional character, despite the fact that Chandler's creation was a private eye.

With his partner Hatch, he went to work on the Sorenson case with a thoroughness that was well known both to his superiors and some men within the grim walls of San Quentin. Unless the coroner advised that the cause of death was a natural one, he considered that the circumstances warranted the closest attention. He examined the premises where the victim had met his end and determined a number of things to his satisfaction. One of them was the interesting fact that Sorenson had apparently entertained at least four different women at the house where he lived with Miss Dorothy Abrams. The other women of whom he found evidence could have been the overnight guests of the owner, but he very much doubted it.

On the second full day of his investigation he visit-

ed the office where Sorenson had worked and was
slightly surprised to find that his successor had already been installed. A few minutes' conversation
with that gentleman convinced him that some foot-
prints were being neatly covered up. He countered
by inviting the young woman who had been Sorenson's secretary to lunch. She accepted gladly and at
once, before her new boss could flash her a signal to
the contrary. By the time that the espresso had been
served, Marlow had found his guest to be a fountain
of information, much of it definitely usable.

"I want you to understand," she said, "that I
don't discuss my boss's business outside the office.
That's an absolute taboo at our company. However,
Mr. Sorenson is dead now, and you are a police
officer checking on the circumstances. That makes it
a different ball game. Ask me what you need to
know, and if I can answer you, I will."

"Fair enough," Marlow conceded. "Anything
you tell me will remain confidential if there's any
way to keep it that way. What I mean is, I won't
repeat anything unless I have to."

"I understand."

"How did Mr. Sorenson treat you?"

"Well enough. He tried awfully hard to make me,
and he promised me some pretty nice things if I
would go to bed with him, but I don't believe in
mixing pleasure with business. And to be honest, I
didn't like him that much. He was too much of a
professional smoothy."

"Do you think that he always tried to handle his

clients' accounts in their best interests?"

She almost laughed at him. "Of course he didn't. Every now and then he had some stock to unload, and then he would get on the telephone and sell it all to people who believed in him."

"Did many of them lose money?"

"Oh, a lot did, some of them large amounts. I know of one client who came in with a hundred and twenty thousand dollars he wanted to invest, not speculate. Three years later, his account was down to less than thirty thousand."

"That's a pretty heavy loss," Marlow said.

"I know it, and he wasn't the only one. But of course Mr. Sorenson made a great deal in commissions. The oftener he could persuade a client to trade, the more he made. And he was very persuasive."

"But you continued to work for him."

"Yes, because the pay is very good, and of course I'm not involved with the market trading in any way."

"Do you have any brokers in your shop whom you consider really honest and capable? Any who you would let handle your own money?"

"Yes, Mr. Jarvis is very honest. One time Mr. Sorenson wanted him to push some Pacific Oil Exploration and he refused. He said that it was a lousy investment and he wouldn't do it."

"How are Mr. Jarvis' sales compared to the other brokers?"

"Very good, he's second in the office in volume.

But he has more clients than most of the men."

By the time that he dropped the young woman back at her office, Marlow had an increasingly clear picture of the man whose death he was investigating. He also understood why a number of people might have wished to have seen him out of the way. That thought was largely subjective until he returned to his office and put in a call to the county coroner. He had learned from experience that he could attach a high degree of credibility to anything he got from that source.

The conversation he held was not a long one, but it was definite. He was told that the cause of death had been electrocution. Otherwise, the deceased had been in excellent physical condition with no significant pathology. One more detail was added. He had recently had sexual intercourse, probably more than once, but that was in no way a contributory cause of death—unless an irate husband had happened on the scene.

A whole atticful of difficulties blew away as soon as he had that information. He simply had not been able to accept the idea that a physically sound man in his early thirties had dropped dead in the shower, particularly when he had just risen from his bed. He called Hatch, who was buried in a mountain of paper work, and with him went out to the canyon house to which he now had a key. On the way there he did some thinking, with the result that the first thing he did was to check all of the electric clocks to see whether or not their telltales had turned from white to red. He found five clocks that all told the same story. He picked up the phone and dialed the number for the correct time. His watch was almost exactly one minute slow. Allowing for that he checked the clocks once more. Taking an average reading, he satisfied himself that the current had been interrupted for only a very brief time. But a few seconds would have been enough.

It took him more than forty minutes to find the place where the flexible cable had been tapped. He missed it the first time, but when he rechecked his work in that highly unlikely location, he found it. As soon as he had done so, he went into the house and phoned for lab help and a police electrician.

The wiring expert confirmed his findings. "This is absolutely a new one on me," he admitted, "and pretty close to foolproof. You know the familiar hazard of having a radio, or something like that, fall into bathwater. Normally water pipes are good grounds, but whoever energized the hot water side got results without ever entering the house and probably without even being seen. It was damn tricky, because there is probably some way that the water heater itself prevented a direct ground. In any event, it obviously worked. Someone knows some very special dirty tricks."

"Where would he learn them?"

"Possibly in the CIA, but I would think the KGB much more likely. The Red Chinese could have dreamed it up. The British are also very good at such technical matters." The police expert shook his head to emphasize his point. "Your man is handy with tools. The rewrapping of the flexible conduit was beautifully done. A month from now, with ordinary corrosion and dirt, it would have been almost invisible."

Marlow made a careful entry in his notebook. "What you are saying is, we are dealing with a professional."

"Hell, yes," the electrician agreed, "and one who has had some very sophisticated training. An experienced intelligence agent, or something very close to that."

John Harbizon went back to his office to check his mail and messages, if any. He had spread quite a wide net through various law enforcement channels, knowing that to go much further he would need some outside help. In addition, the reward posted by the city of Boylesport might produce some results, though he tended to doubt it. At best, it might serve to loosen the tongues of otherwise reluctant witnesses. There were a lot of people who were willing to get involved for ten thousand dollars.

He parked his car in the available slot that by unstated precedence was his and went inside. His mind was full of the California thing. He knew very little about it, and he wanted to get all that he could despite the distance.

There was a message to call Lieutenant Walchewski at the NYPD.

A Mr. Henry O'Connor wanted him to call. He

didn't know the name.

Investigator Elliott, also of the NYPD, wanted to talk with him.

And Investigator Phil Marlow, LAPD, wanted him to call as soon as convenient.

The desk man who handed him his messages had one more item. "There's a young woman here to see you. I put her in the reception area. She seemed quite upset. I told her that I didn't know when you would be in, but she decided to wait for you anyway." He checked a slip of paper. "She's a Miss Helen Chow."

Harbizon managed to keep any unusual expression off his face, which was a minor achievement. He took his messages and then went to the washroom for a few moments before he did anything else. He was vain enough to comb his hair and brush his sleeves with the palms of his hands before he left the room. Having done the best that he could for himself on short notice, he went to the small reception area and found Helen Chow. He had anticipated that she would be upset; the circumstances of her visit indicated that, and very obviously she was. But that did not rob her of her dignity, and when she rose to speak to him, he reacted in her favor because he couldn't help himself.

"Lieutenant, I want to see you very much if I may," she said.

Damn right she could see him, but he was careful not to let that show. Instead he welcomed her formally and led the way to his office. There he provid-

ed a hard chair, the best one available, and asked if
he could get her anything. Most of the stuff in the
few machines was terrible, but there were canned
soft drinks and coffee. "No thank you," she responded. "I just need to talk with you."

As she sat down, Harbizon closed the door. He
prepared himself for anything from an appeal to
leave her alone to a full confession. He only knew
that she would not have come all of the way to
Boylesport without an appointment for something
trivial. He sat down behind his desk and put on his
most sympathetic manner. "What can I do for you?"
he asked.

She folded her hands in her lap and looked at him
steadily. "I'm about to destroy completely any re-
spect that you may have for me," she said quite
candidly. "You can't think very much of me in the
first place, since I admit to having been William San
Marco's mistress."

"You had a reason," Harbizon heard himself saying. "Throughout history a good many other young
women have done the same thing. For king and
country—and all that."

Helen Chow eyed him from under lowered
lashes. He could not read her expression. "You're
being overly generous. I've also had sex at times
simply because I wanted to. I am not a babe in arms,
lieutenant."

"You didn't come here to tell me that."

"No, I didn't." She composed herself and
smoothed her skirt over her crossed knees. Someone

had once remarked to Harbizon that Oriental girls
had crooked legs; it had been a slander.

"Lieutenant, on the night that San Marco was
killed, I was with Harold—Harold Horowitz. We
had dinner together."

"You mentioned that last time."

"I know that I did. I also told you that we were
together most of the night—and that we could produce witnesses."

Harbizon was well ahead of her then. Dietrich
had already told him that Horowitz's alibi hadn't
held up. The promised witnesses had not appeared.
So now the girl had come, sensing that he was interested in her enough to take more than casual notice,
hoping to make a confession and thereby enlist his
sympathy. But he kept his face under control and
appeared to be all considerate attention.

"I can tell you where we ate, and the staff will
remember me."

"Perhaps it would be a good idea to do that."

She reacted to the hardening of his attitude as
though she had been expecting it. But she did not
allow it to show in her voice. "Harold is Jewish and
I am Chinese. We share a common heritage in one
thing . . . a close attention to matters concerning
money. While we ate, Harold had an interesting
idea to suggest to me. First, he was considering
dropping his orthodox faith in order to marry me.
He put that in the form of an announcement."

Harbizon took a moment or two. "As I remember
it," he said, "you were quite anxious to marry him,

and only the religious problem was keeping you apart."

Helen lit a cigarette with careful ease. Harbizon did not smoke, so he had no light to offer her. As she blew the first lungful out of her mouth in a thin stream, he wished that she would stop the habit. It disturbed him.

"At one time that might have been true, but Harold has been a great deal more self-centered lately. To the point of forgetting to ask whether or not I wanted him to make such a sacrifice."

"I see."

"Anyhow, he had a suggestion. He reminded me that I had allowed an unspeakable person to take me to bed with him. After that he made his proposal . . . that I accept a very limited number of lovers, each at a very high fee, and that we then invest my earnings together. Harold works in Wall Street—I told you that. He had an uncle who was a financial wizard. According to Harold this man would take my earnings, if you choose to call them that, and build us a considerable sum on which to get married. He was certain that my exotic appeal would command a premium price."

"Had he ever talked to you like this before?"

"No, never. You should have known the answer to that, lieutenant. You are a detective."

"Meaning that if he had, you would not have gone to dinner with him on that night."

She answered by taking another puff from her cigarette, then she carefully put it out. "I'm sorry," she said. "I see that my smoking bothers you."

"Now you are the detective."

"I would like to think that it was concern for me, rather than the irritation of the smoke itself."

"That's quite true—and I'm not being gallant."

"If you were not a policeman, and I your suspect, it could be quite interesting."

He did not fall for that. "I am a policeman, Helen, and I intend to stay one, despite the very considerable enticement. Now you are going to tell me that you walked out of the restaurant and therefore can't account for any of Mr. Horowitz's actions for the rest of the night."

She nodded, with a certain respectful deference that was as hard to ignore as a salaam. He was a romantic at heart, and the girl before him reminded him of some of the lurid literature he had read as a boy and had found captivating. He turned that off forcefully and came back to reality. "Where were you, after dinner?" he asked.

"I was home—alone. That is the truth, but I can't prove it."

"Did Harold subsequently tell you where he had gone, or what he had done, after he left you?"

"After *I* left *him*, lieutenant. Permanently."

"Did he tell you who his uncle was . . . the man who was to enrich you both?"

"Yes. His name was Simon Korngold. He was killed recently, in a traffic accident."

Harbizon did not allow his face to betray a thing. "Two questions, Helen. Am I right in assuming that you didn't dispose of your former patron, to use the polite term?"

"You put that very graciously, thank you. I didn't kill Bill San Marco."

"Or anyone else?"

"Or anyone else."

"Do you know who did?"

"I have no idea."

Harbizon waited for a moment, not wanting to dismiss her. But he had to. "Thank you for coming to see me," he said.

Helen rose, quietly and gracefully. "Do you believe me?" she asked.

"At the moment I'm inclined to, but that's as far as I can go."

"It's quite enough, lieutenant. I've noticed the way you've been looking at me, and your careful restraint. Are you married?"

"I was."

"Is there a particular girl at the moment?"

"Why?"

"Just asking."

"No, not at the moment." He should not have told her that. It came out before he thought.

"When this is all over, and I am no longer your suspect, perhaps you will let me cook dinner for you, at my apartment. Just dinner, but it might be pleasant."

"I'm sure it would be," he answered her, and then showed her out before he committed himself to anything more. After she had gone, it took him a good ten minutes to get himself fully under control once more.

8

Lieutenant Ted Walchewski was much less composed than he had been the first time that Harbizon had been in his office. At that time he had appeared to be in the position of a man fighting the good fight for the sake of a lost cause. Now what he had lost in composure he had gained in confidence. He had a tight, tense enthusiasm that refused to be held under too much restraint.

"Have you got a good line yet on who killed your stock speculator?" he asked as soon as Harbizon had settled down into a hard chair.

"No," Harbizon answered, "not yet." His tone implied that that was an interim answer, one that would definitely be revised later.

"I'm wishing you all of the luck in the world," Walchewski came back. "Meanwhile, a helluva lot is suddenly going on. You see, there have been four deaths, all by violence, of stock market figures who were big on rimming the public. One might have passed relatively unnoticed, but the sum total of four has put a damn bright spotlight on the whole thing. Schneider and Burroughs, in that column of theirs, have been running a full background on each one, and the composite picture is a real fireworks display."

"I know," Harbizon said. "Since the Lockheim killing, and meeting them, I've been following them daily. Apparently the Korngold death—the traffic victim—took the lid off the worst mess of all."

Walchewski nodded energetically. "It sure as hell did. I know that all the evidence points to accidental death, but it fits too well into the pattern. Now this thing in California—how much do you know about it?"

"I've talked to the man who's handling it out there, an investigator named Marlow. We've compared notes."

"First name Philip?"

"Yes, I think so."

"Does he spell Marlow with an 'e'?"

"I don't know, but he's a cop, not a private eye. To be serious for a moment, he feels that the killing out there was triggered by what has been happening here, but he doesn't think that the same man is responsible."

"Do you agree with that?"

"No, for two reasons. First, the killing was expertly done by an unusual method—one that requires sophisticated training. Secondly, I discount the physical distance. It's a matter of a few hours to go to California, and you can buy a ticket under any name you like."

"But the MO wasn't the same."

"No, it wasn't, but the technique was. It's like a good pianist—if he can play Chopin, he can probably also play Liszt."

Walchewski considered that. "A nice point. And there is another thing: the stock market hotshot. I presume you noticed that of the murder victims—the known murder victims—one was a speculator, one a specialist, and one a broker. And each was as parasitic as they come. This guy in Los Angeles: Marlow found out that he had just put in a big buy order on a sleepy little stock called Wanderlust, Inc. He checked that one out thoroughly. The company is small, decent, and turns out a good product. Sales have been up encouragingly, but not anything to arouse excitement. Shortly before he died, Sorenson, that's the victim, phoned Wanderlust and talked to the president. He was told then that even a few transactions in the stock would have an effect on the price."

Harbizon was ahead of him. "So he intended to tout the stock, thereby shoving it up, and then unload his own holdings before anyone learned what he was doing."

"Exactly. Perfectly legal, probably, but it was a clear case of manipulation. Marlow said that he could have cleared ten grand easily if the deal had gone through."

Harbizon leaned forward. "Ted, don't quote me on this, but there is one aspect of the California thing that I like very much."

"Sorenson wasn't Jewish."

Harbizon moved Walchewski up another notch in his esteem. "Exactly. I've been spending some time with the FBI looking at the anti-Semitic lunacy fringe. Now, if the California thing can be tied in, that lead goes up the flue, thank God."

Walchewski let a few seconds pass, then changed the subject. "I've got some developments for you you may not know about. Indirect, but interesting. One: there is a sharpie who has been making his living for some time devising tax dodges and shelters for the very rich. He is Jewish, incidentally, and the interesting thing is, he has applied for police protection."

"Are you going to give it to him?"

"Are you nuts? He worked a lot with Lockheim, and now he is genuinely scared. He thinks it is a Red group of anti-Semites that is doing all this. Against the capitalistic system and down on his people. He has asked the FBI, his legislative representative, and the SEC to investigate."

"What happens if they investigate him?"

"I'd like to be around to see that. There's more. The SEC has put out a release about stricter controls to be imposed on stock transactions in the near future. The brokerage houses are in agony. The new commodity regulating commission is flexing its muscles, and it should—that business is gambling pure and simple no matter how much they call it speculation. Personally, I think they should slam the door on the whole thing. And some very interesting reform bills are being rushed onto the floor of Congress."

"They did not die in vain, then."

"No, apparently they didn't, though I won't say that publicly. But I will say this to you—if there is one more killing, and it's another rip-off artist, then everything will hit the fan for sure."

"Do you think that's a possibility?" Harbizon asked.

"What's your guess?"

"I'm expecting it at any time," he admitted.

In California Phil Marlow was talking with Mrs. Betty Williamson, whose stock account had diminished drastically while it was in the hands of Williams, Sloan, Furman & Brown. She was an intelligent woman who knew how to express herself clearly when she was giving an official statement.

"For a while," she said, "I wasn't unduly alarmed, largely because Mr. Rampole called me very frequently and reassured me that I did not need to worry. I should explain, sergeant, that at that time I regarded my stockbroker in the same light as I regard my attorney, or for that matter anyone else whom I turn to for advice and counsel. For example, Mr. Sorelli at the bank."

"Did Mr. Sorelli ever advise you concerning your stock holdings?"

"Only indirectly. I told him, not too long ago, where I had my account and asked his opinion. He told me, rather cautiously now that I recall our conversation, that I was with a reputable brokerage firm, but he strongly advised that I stay in blue chips. Therefore, when Mr. Rampole called me about Pacific Oil Exploration I asked him if it was a blue chip, and he told me that it was even better. He talked about the continuing energy crisis and said that he felt that company would be one of the saviors of our economy. So I invested as he advised."

"And lost your shirt," Marlow said, without thinking.

Mrs. Williamson did not let it throw her. "Yes, I lost quite heavily, and you understand, sergeant, I didn't want to speculate—I wanted to *invest*. In sound, secure stocks."

"You made that clear to the broker?"

"By letter, at the time that I opened my account. And I have a carbon."

"Excellent! After you became disenchanted with Mr. Rampole, then Mr. Sorenson took over your account, is that right?"

"Yes, he told me he would handle it personally, and he implied that he would recover what I had lost very quickly. I did gain almost two hundred dollars that month, but of course that isn't very much in light of what I have lost."

"Do you still own your Pacific Oil Exploration stock?"

"Yes, I do."

Mrs. Williamson was the seventh Ben Sorenson client Marlow had interviewed, and the picture that each had painted was the same. Every one of them had been ruthlessly exploited. When he thanked Mrs. Williamson and went outside, he wondered if he really wanted to catch the man who had so neatly eliminated Ben Sorenson and had removed him from his place of public trust and confidence. But murder was murder, and he knew that he would go on with his investigation until he hit pay dirt, unless he were pulled off the case for some as yet unforeseeable reason.

John Harbizon was grateful for the fact that his abilities were respected and he was kept free of pressure from up above. Consequently, when the chief asked him to come in, he knew he had no cause for concern.

In that he was right. The chief made that clear immediately and put him at his ease. "Have you got anything definite yet?" he asked, simply as a conversational gambit.

Harbizon shook his head. "I'm at that stage when I'm doing all the plodding work and praying for a break. I'm getting some help in running down known car bombers who might be involved. Running ex-Intelligence agents is a much harder job, but I do have one man in my sights. He was in Intelligence work, and he's a stockbroker."

"Any other connection?"

"Yes, he got badly burned by Lockheim and his manipulations, but against that is the fact that he is a very solid citizen, he checks out all the way, and dozens of people will vouch for him."

"Alibi?"

"Nothing that can be solidly checked. Incidental-

ly, he offered to take a polygraph test if I wanted him
to. He understands the situation, and he is fully
aware that he has both technique, presumably, and
motive."

"Usually the innocent invite polygraph tests," the
chief said, stating what they both knew, "the guilty
refuse them."

"I considered that."

"Anyone else?"

"Yes, I'm very interested in an aggressive young
man named Harold Horowitz. He works in Wall
Street and has a Chinese girlfriend who at one time
was the mistress of that man who was killed up in
Westchester County."

"Is she the one who came to see you here?"

"Yes. She's quite a principled young lady, as a
matter of fact."

The chief eyed him. "You seem a little defensive
on that point."

Harbizon had no choice but to admit it. "I am,"
he conceded. "And I might as well add that she has
given me a wide opening for social contact—after
this is all over."

"That's quite interesting, John. Are you going to
follow through?"

"I haven't made up my mind yet."

"I didn't see her," the chief said, "but those who
did were impressed."

Harbizon handled that easily. "You would have
been too. She's quite something, and at the risk of
being caught out again, she isn't promiscuous—I've

had a check run. She's offered me dinner at her apartment—dinner only."

"Is she an active suspect?"

"I don't think so. It doesn't add up, and if the California thing is related, she was here at the time. The account she gave me of her relationship with William San Marco, the murder victim in Westchester, is accurate. I've interviewed several of his friends, and he complained to them that his very expensive mistress wasn't putting out."

The chief thought for a moment. "I think you should cultivate her," he said.

Harbizon was cautious. "Just on general principles?" he asked.

"No, for practical reasons. If you've been fortunate enough to catch the young lady's eye, then she might prove to be a valuable witness. In my experience ladies who have changed their affections frequently become quite talkative. I've been reading your reports, and I know about her boyfriend who tried to make her a call girl. Incidentally, how about his connection with the traffic victim, I believe his name was Korngold?"

"Coincidence, as I see it. I've been in close touch with Elliott of the NYPD, and he is convinced that it was a felony hit and run and nothing more. There was no way that the man who killed Korngold could have known that he would leave the trading floor before the end of the session. And there's no connection at all between the driver and Korngold."

"The driver could have been hired, but I agree

that it looks very much like a coincidence that Korngold was killed. He was a viper, I understand."

Harbizon nodded. "Like *The Mikado,* none of the
victims will be missed."

"A point," the chief said, then he broke off the
conversation.

Robert Jarvis was willing to talk. He arrived
promptly at the place Marlow had suggested, a bar
in the valley well away from the offices of Williams,
Sloan, Furman & Brown in Beverly Hills. He shook
hands and then sat down in a quiet booth to face the
inquisition that he knew was coming.

Marlow led up to it carefully. "Mr. Jarvis, your
name was given to me as a strictly honest stockbroker in what was Ben Sorenson's office. Is it true that
you refused to push Pacific Oil Exploration onto
your clients when you were asked to do so?"

Jarvis was uncomfortable with the question and
took some seconds before he answered it. "Yes,
that's true, because I knew that it was a potential
bad loser. And that's how it turned out."

"Your company had a position in the stock and
wanted to unload, is that right?"

"Yes."

"Does this sort of thing happen often?"

"Every day."

Marlow asked a number of additional questions
and warmed his man up for what was to come. He
was satisfied that Jarvis was an unusually honest
person, honest enough that he obviously did not

want to embarrass his employer any more than was necessary. When the time was right, Marlow dug in.

"Mr. Jarvis, since you've been in this business for a long time, how do you rate your late boss? How did he compare with other men in similar positions?"

Jarvis considered that carefully. "He was a very good salesmen," he began, "and he certainly appealed to the women. Many of his clients were female. You already know that he was very fond of the ladies, and he had a great many affairs."

"Were any of his clients also his mistresses?"

"I don't think so. Most of his female clients were well past the point of being attractive as bed partners. Ben was very discreet. He had to be."

"Would you describe him as a good financial adviser?"

That brought a dead stop, and Marlow wondered if he had gone too fast too soon. Then Jarvis answered him. "Ben and I often disagreed on the value of certain securities. Of course, that is to be expected. I will say, though, that I was right a little more often than he was. In particular, there was one stock he was pushing while I was almost certain that it was being manipulated and, therefore, was dangerous. Some of his clients lost very badly, although Sphinx Wire and Cable is, basically, a good company. But that often means very little when the speculators step in."

Because he was a complete professional at his job,

John Harbizon did not shrink from the meticulously detailed investigation work that any difficult major case entailed. He also knew that good hard thinking was a large part of any successful operation of that type, and he was not the kind of man to substitute impulsive judgments for careful analysis. For that reason he sat alone in his house at nine o'clock in the evening refusing the enticements of the TV. Anyway, he was fed up with being sung to by car salesmen. Finally, when he was reasonably sure of his ground, he picked up the phone and dialed the chief's private number. After brief preliminaries he said, "I think I would like to go to Los Angeles and confer with this man Marlow of the LAPD. I've been giving the matter some thought, and I believe I see a connection."

"If it will help, by all means go," the chief told him immediately. "Strictly off the record, I'm glad you made that decision. The council will be pleased to see the evidence of extended action. So will the mayor. A lot of the citizens keep calling in to ask what is being done."

"I understand," Harbizon told him. "But this is strictly business. I'm not packing any sun tan lotion."

"Do whatever is necessary," the chief concluded. "Just keep me in the picture if you learn anything."

"Depend on that," Harbizon said, and hung up. He called TWA and made a reservation for Los Angeles at four the following afternoon. He still had one important thing to do before he left, and he wanted to allow as much time as he might need.

Bert Schneider was in and waiting when he got there the following morning. The reporter offered coffee which was several grades superior to the product available to New York's finest, and he made small talk until his partner arrived. Burroughs came in within the next five minutes, and the meeting was able to get down to business.

"I saw your column on the front page this morning," Harbizon began. "I read it coming in on the train. This whole business must have been an indirect boost for you."

"It has been indeed," Burroughs agreed. "We had been interested in the stock market for some time as a fertile field for some investigative reporting when Lockheim was blown up. We already knew about him, and about San Marco. So when San Marco got his, our readership jumped way up in the continuing surveys. It's still climbing."

"Did you get any reaction from the Korngold thing?" Harbizon asked.

"Yes," Schneider responded, "very much so. It damn near made us as big as Woodward and Bernstein in Washington. We had been gathering material on the Sphinx Wire and Cable fraud—and that's the word for it—when we ran across Korngold. We latched onto him and we had a thick folder full of good stuff when he bought the farm. So all we had to do was to put it into the typewriter."

"How many more are there like him?" Harbizon

asked.

Burroughs shook his head. "Here in New York a whole nest full. Around the country a few more, but the majority of the worst manipulators operate off the floor of the exchange. In that way they don't have to pay commissions."

"Now I've got a big question," Harbizon prefaced. "Think before you answer it. A stockbroker was erased in Los Angeles, you know all about that . . ."

"Yes, we do," Schneider cut in, a little too quickly. His partner picked up the ball. "Off the record," he said, "we're on that right now. We think there may be a connection, and to be honest about it, we're hoping to break the story."

"And you see me as a possible hazard to that," Harbizon supplied.

"Yes, in a way. You see, we're both investigating the same thing. Only we don't have police powers."

"And I don't have the power of the press," Harbizon added. "I'll make you a deal. Why don't we try to help each other. You're good at digging up things, and I understand your desire to break any important news in your column. Insofar as I can, ethically, I'll return any favors. I can't be more specific than that, and you know why."

"It's a deal," Schneider said immediately. "And if you like, we'll make our first contribution right now."

Harbizon looked at Gene Burroughs who nodded. "What have you got?" he asked.

Schneider answered. "First, the killing on the Coast was a very cute job, using a little-known technique. It wasn't an ordinary homicide."

"I know that," Harbizon said, "but how did you find it out?"

"Probably the same way that you did," Burroughs answered. "By having friends in the business. We make a lot of long-distance calls."

Schneider went on. "For a while we were hot on the Jewish angle. I'm Jewish, and naturally we were both very concerned."

"So was I," Harbizon admitted. "Dietrich and I have been checking out all of the crackpot organizations and individuals who might be trying to start World War III. So far we haven't turned up any positive leads. Now the Sorenson death, if I can establish that it's related, shoots that angle down, thank God. Sorenson was his real name, and he wasn't Jewish."

The two columnists looked at each other, then Schneider spoke for them both. "Two things that might help you. First of all, there is a heavyweight financial adviser who knows a lot of important people in Washington. For some time he has been conducting a quiet campaign to have the rules of the New York Stock Exchange, and the work of the SEC, overhauled and made a lot less favorable to speculators. If they want to gamble, let 'em go to the horse races, that was his attitude. We discovered that he is an old friend of the president of Sphinx Wire and Cable."

"I missed that," Harbizon admitted.

"You met him, then?" Burroughs asked.

"Yes, Cecil Forrester. I interviewed him. I also know that he put some of his clients in that stock and they lost a bundle."

"Do you know why?" Schneider asked.

"You tell me."

"Sphinx is a good sound outfit—we've been out there and talked with the top people. They're highly capable, and they know what they're doing. Their financial position is very sound and the order backlog is substantial. The products check out as superior. So all the way it should be a good investment, if you go by the fundamentals. But Lockheim and San Marco got together, and between them they screwed everybody. The stock went down the tube for no valid reason, and a lot of good people got hurt. Lockheim made a mint, and undoubtedly San Marco did too. Forrester and his clients took it on the chin."

Harbizon came to the point. "Are you suggesting that Forrester was responsible for correcting this situation—either personally or indirectly?"

"That would be accusing a man of murder," Burroughs answered immediately, "and we're not about to do that. Another thing—he's been working through legal channels and he has a lot of clout, and so do his clients. He handles some very big portfolios, and the people who own them often make substantial campaign contributions. What we are saying is that he is prominent in the scenario. He may be keeping a few things to himself."

"Not guilty knowledge," Schneider added, "but informative, you might say."

Harbizon made a note. "If I find out anything interesting on the Coast and I can, I'll let you in on it," he promised, thereby easing his conscience. He had offered a deal and he would have to hold up his end.

"When are you going out there?" Schneider asked.

"Later this afternoon. I want to see if I can establish a firmer connection than I have now. By the way, can you offhand think of any person or persons who might be likely victims in the future if this thing continues? Any conspicuous candidates for elimination in the class of San Marco or Lockheim?"

Burroughs shook his head. "Lots of candidates, too many, but not anyone conspicuous."

"Would you say that Lockheim and San Marco were conspicuous?"

"Within the financial community, yes. A lot of people knew about them." Burroughs looked at his partner who turned his head sideways a bare fraction of an inch. Harbizon was not looking at him, but he still caught the movement.

"Of course, San Marco could have been eliminated by the husband or boyfriend of one of his conquests," Harbizon said easily. "He was a hell of a womanizer."

"And how," Burroughs agreed. "He was a rapist too, but he beat the rap. The funny thing is, he was never attractive to women. He got it when he bought it, and no other way. He spent a fortune on his women. We know about one mistress of his who took him to the cleaners for a very round sum and gave him almost nothing back. He had it coming. He had damn near ruined someone in her family."

Harbizon kept his face very still and for a moment watched his breathing. "Then we have to consider that his involvement in Sphinx Wire and Cable may have been a coincidence."

The columnists exchanged open glances, and then Schneider spoke for the team. "That's possible, yes, but the odds are way against it. We do have something that you may not know, and as we see it it's damn important."

Harbizon was fully attentive. "What is it?" he asked.

"The man who was killed in Los Angeles, Sorenson was his name, was into Sphinx Wire and Cable up to his neck."

9

The West Valley Police Station in Los Angeles had a considerable spread of green grass in front and a large parking lot in the rear with plenty of room for the attached personnel to leave their private cars. When he saw it Harbizon was slightly envious, but not on his own behalf. His office in Boylesport was not too bad, but the facilities provided in New York were not worthy of the men and women who were asked to work in them. He went inside, showed his credentials at the desk, and asked to see Phil Marlow.

Marlow and Hatch both came out to meet him. As they went down the corridor together to the coffee room, Harbizon sized up his opposite number. Marlow was of average size, with thinning sandy hair and a slightly round face that could be either cherubic or stone hard as the circumstances might require. He wore a brown suit that might have stood a pressing, but it was of high quality, and had come from the hands of a good tailor, or else a first-class men's shop.

Hatch was taller by two or three inches, dark-haired, and well muscled. He was clearly a physical type, but that aspect was subdued by a patina of obvious education and training in his profession. Harbizon felt better almost at once. He had been fortunate in Dietrich, and now it was clear that the West Coast situation was in good hands.

As soon as they were seated and Hatch had produced three cups of coffee from a convenient machine, Harbizon opened up. "I came out here to see you because I think the Sorenson killing is tied in with two homicides I'm investigating back home."

Marlow responded to that as though they had known each other for some time. He spoke deliberately, because that was his style. "We've been operating up to now on the theory that your homicides may have triggered the one we have. You know how that works. Also, the MO's are entirely different, and Sorenson doesn't fit the pattern of your two victims."

Harbizon used the device of beginning with agreement. "I had the same idea, until I got something else just before I left. Sorenson was heavily into a stock that was closely tied to my two victims. I realize that we have three different MO's, but they're alike in that they are all tricky and show an expert's hand. Look at it the other way, so many homicides are routine affairs—family quarrels, shootings, you name it—but how often do we get one that is in the assassination category? Not very often. Now we have three of them, and all three victims were stock market operators heavily involved in the same security."

"Looking at it that way," Hatch said, "I can see why you came out here. Suppose you fill us in on your end of this thing."

In careful, well-organized detail Harbizon described the killings of Nathan Lockheim and William San Marco and his subsequent investigation. He told them about Dietrich's work and about the apparently accidental death of Simon Korngold, the one that had done the most to trigger a massive reaction against many of the existing stock market practices. He filled in the several items of information that had not been made public. When he had finished he had told it all, including what he knew of Harold Horowitz and the pertinent details concerning Helen Chow. He didn't tell of her call on him at his office.

"All right," Marlow said. "Here's what we've got at this end." He told his own story with equal care and thoroughness, laying out the principal points of investigative interest and soft-pedaling those which were of background value only. Before he finished Harbizon had confirmed his earlier judgment that Marlow was a top man. Hatch had remained silent most of the time, which was probably good judgment on his part.

When the recital was over, Hatch got the full file on the Sorenson investigation and gave it to Harbizon to read. That task took the rest of the morning. He was still hard at it when Hatch came in to ask him if he would like some lunch.

When he returned to the police station, there was a message for him. Sergeant Dietrich of the New York State Police wanted him to call. Harbizon got on the line, gave his credit card number, and was talking to Dietrich almost at once. "What have you got?" he asked.

"You asked me to check on Cecil Forrester, your financial adviser friend. On the day that Lockheim was blown up there is no way to prove conclusively where he was. Reportedly he was in his office, but his secretary was out sick that day and it seems he had no visitors. Don't say anything, I know what you're thinking. But he's definitely out of the San Marco thing. On that night Forrester was delivering an address to a women's club in Jamaica. So forget it. I know that it was a long shot, John, but he did have motive and presumably the techniques."

"He could have hired someone," Harbizon suggested.

"I doubt it. In the first place, he would have had to hire someone to commit murder, and it isn't that easy. He would lay himself open to blackmail for the rest of his life if the killer got away. If he didn't, he would have to stand trial for murder himself. No way."

"I was thinking of one of his Intelligence pals. Someone who, perhaps, owed him a favor."

"Possibly, but you'd have a helluva time proving it."

Harbizon thanked him and hung up. He had not placed much faith in the idea of Forrester in the first place, but it was, or had been, a visible lead, and he didn't intend to overlook anything.

He spent two hours of the afternoon with Marlow and Hatch discussing the whole matter with very little productive result, other than the fact that they understood each other thoroughly and agreed to co-ordinate efforts as long as the case remained open and active.

Marlow summed up how things stood on the West Coast in very simple, clear English. "First, we don't know who totaled out Sorenson. Secondly, even if we did, we'd have one helluva time proving it. As of right now we have no witnesses. We don't have a single lead to go on. We know that the man was handy with tools, which cuts the suspects down to about twenty million or so. There are a lot of good mechanics around. We learned that Sorenson had had some married women at that isolated canyon house, but no enraged husbands are in the picture. He had a woman there the night before he was killed, but we haven't any idea of her identity, and she isn't likely to come forward."

"Informants?" Harbizon asked.

"Nothing. Zero. This wasn't the kind of thing that gets out on the street. We've talked to every canyon resident for more than a mile in both directions. Blank. Nobody saw anything, and in this instance I believe them. So where do we go from here?"

"I have one suggestion," Harbizon said. "If we are right in assuming that the three killings are related, then the motive lies in Sorenson's stock market activities, not in his womanizing."

"That's logical," Hatch conceded.

"Then there are the people who lost money through him, but narrowed down, perhaps, to those who lost on Sphinx Wire and Cable. There can't be too many of those, not with a single broker."

"We're hitting that right now," Marlow said. "I grant that we haven't been concentrating on Sphinx, because we still entertain the idea that the Sorenson killing may have been triggered by your New York jobs. But we will look at the Sphinx investors very closely, and we'll keep you posted."

They ended it for the day. Harbizon went back to his motel and was on the point of checking out and heading toward the airport when the idea hit him. He didn't know where it came from, only that it was suddenly there, like Minerva, full grown and ready for battle. He sat down and forced himself to think, to make sure that he was not about to run off half cocked. When he had satisfied himself that he knew what he was doing, he took out his notebook, checked a number, and called Forrester's office in New York.

Because of the time difference the office was closed, but an answering service came on the line— possibly in response to Harbizon's prayer. He identified himself and asked to be put through to Mr. Forrester at home, saying that it was urgent. The authority of his position got him through, and within a minute he had the financial adviser on the line.

He identified himself and told him that he was speaking from Los Angeles. "I have just had a brainstorm, Mr. Forrester," he said, "and I want to ask your immediate cooperation."

"Anything I can do," Forrester responded.

"All right, sir. You know the financial community, and certainly you are familiar with the Sphinx Wire and Cable stock and how it has been manipulated."

"To my sorrow."

"This is in very strict confidence, but so far the police investigation hasn't turned up very much that will help us to end this thing. I'm now convinced that we have three killings all related to that particular stock, and all three victims used it to their profit. So my question is: Who is left that might be the *next* victim? Are there any more people who have been conspicuous in manipulating the Sphinx Wire and Cable stock? Anywhere in the country?"

Forrester saw it immediately. "I understand. I can't give you a list offhand, but I could call you back in an hour if that will be all right."

Harbizon gave the number of the motel, and his room, while a sense of impending excitement grew within him. Forrester could well be the best man in the country to forecast who might be the next on someone's list, and now that he was out of it himself, he could be safely consulted.

Forty-two minutes later the phone rang in Harbizon's room. He picked it up with his notebook open and his pen already in his hand.

"I've thought carefully," Forrester told him, "and I made one or two calls to people whom I completely trust without telling them a thing. I have a total of eleven names to give to you. In one case, all three of us nominated one individual. All the others got one vote each."

"Give me the runners-up first," Harbizon said. He listened and wrote the names down, with addresses for each one. When he had done that, he asked for the name that had gotten all three votes.

"He's a man in Chicago," Forrester said. "He publishes one of the many tip sheets that are put out, usually for about two hundred dollars a year. He's in the self-fulfilling prophecy business. When he touts something it often goes up or down as a result, whichever way he predicts. He makes his real money by riding his own forecasts, and enough people follow him to cause a predictable fluctuation. Of course he only does this with smaller firms—he never plays with anything like General Motors or DuPont."

"Was he in the Sphinx thing?"

"He certainly was, and possibly still is. As I hear it, he boosted it to the skies, helped to get it run up, and then sold short. When it came down many of his clients lost heavily, but he made a pile."

Harbizon was a calm man, but his pen almost shook as he held it over the paper. "What's his name?" he asked.

"Irving W. Brown. As I said, he's in Chicago, but I only have a post office box address."

Chicago was soaked in rain. It came down out of a gray sky that shrouded the city at low altitude from horizon to horizon. Air traffic was severely restricted, and during most of the day the airports were closed. When Harbizon's flight finally managed to get in, it was early evening and the rain had not relented. The few available cabs were themselves water-soaked, and the street traffic was constantly tied up by accidents.

It had been Harbizon's intention to go first to the police facility nearest to the post office where Brown had his box, but the almost impossible driving conditions caused him to change his mind. He resorted to the telephone and made a number of calls. There was no Irving W. Brown listed in the directory, but he had expected that. By the time he had finished, he had formally notified the Chicago Police Department that he was in its jurisdiction, and he had ferreted out his subject's telephone number. He called it and waited while the phone rang for some time. Finally he was rewarded by an abrupt, "Yes?"

"Mr. Brown?"

"What is it?"

"This is Lieutenant Harbizon of the Boylesport, New York, Police Department."

"Who gave you my number?"

Harbizon bore down a little harder. "Mr. Brown, I've come to Chicago expressly to see you. It's very important that I do so as soon as possible."

"I don't see anybody. I'm too busy. Sorry." He hung up.

Harbizon called him back and waited patiently for almost twenty rings until Brown at last came back on the line. At that point he wasted no more time. *"Mr. Brown, you'd better see me immediately if you want to keep on living."* His voice carried full, urgent authority.

"Are you threatening me?"

"No, sir, I'm trying to warn you. You may be in very acute danger, as of this minute."

Brown softened very slightly. "Tell me about it."

"Not over the phone, but I will come and see you. Give me your address."

"You haven't proven to me who you are."

"I'll show you my full credentials when I get there. Is there a doorman at your building?"

"Yes."

"I'll show them to him too, before I come up."

There was a pause. "All right, I'll see you sometime after nine-thirty—not before. I have to go out first."

"Nine-thirty," Harbizon repeated. "I'll be there. What's your address?"

Brown supplied it and specified the twenty-third floor. That automatically told Harbizon that it would be an exclusive and expensive apartment, in all probability somewhere near to the lake shore.

When he had finished phoning he went to the airport police facility where he was able to consult a map of the city. As soon as he located his destination, he saw that his deduction had been correct. It was south of the Loop area and less than a quarter mile from the lake. Presumably Brown had a nice view of the water on clear days.

Because of the weather conditions, the airport police advised him to go into town via the limo service and then catch a cab, if he could, downtown. That made sense, and Harbizon rode in a seat by himself, with much almost continuous splashing and occasional skidding, into the central part of the city. When he got there he discovered that he was hungry. He checked his watch and then chose a quick-service restaurant where he ate a not very satisfactory dinner. Unfortunately, he was used to that, and insofar as food went, Chicago was little different from other major cities.

When he had finished he checked the time once more, considered the still drenching rain, and decided not to wait any longer. He could not predict how long it might take him to reach the fashionable address he had been given, and getting a cab was probably going to be a problem.

It proved to be a worse one than he had anticipated. He tried from under a canopy for a while with no luck at all. One or two cabs did come by, but they were grabbed by others who had been out waiting in the street despite the continuing downpour. Resigning himself, he stood out in the street himself, with no protection from the rain, and tried to keep his patience. He was there nearly twenty minutes until two cabs appeared almost together. Someone else rushed out and flagged the first. He got the second.

As he sat miserably in the back, Harbizon was

still grateful that he was out of the weather for a little while at least. He would have a short dash into the building which wouldn't matter, and presumably the doorman would be able to get him a cab when it came time to leave. The worst was behind him. He planned what he was going to say to Brown.

He was not watching outside—he had seen enough of that for one night, when he felt the cab coming to a stop. He leaned forward and saw the tall building that was undoubtedly his destination a good block ahead. "Something wrong?" he asked.

Before the driver could answer a uniformed policeman bulking large in his rain gear loomed beside the car. "You'll have to stop here," he said.

Harbizon rolled the window down so that he could speak. "What's the problem?" he asked.

"Police road block," the man outside answered, and turned away.

"Wait!" Harbizon called. When the patrolman turned back, he held up his badge. "Does this help?" he asked. "I've already reported in."

The officer took it for a moment and then handed it back. "All right," he said. "Go ahead."

The driver fed gas, the cab moved, and for a few more precious seconds of relative dryness Harbizon was inside. There was a canopy over the entranceway that provided some shelter. The driver pulled under it, moving around at least two police cars that were flashing rotating blue lights into the soaked, unimpressed night. Harbizon handed the driver a five and saw him pick up another passenger almost immediately. It was a good night for hacking.

A plainclothes policeman in a plastic raincoat confronted Harbizon. "How did you get through?" he asked. Once more Harbizon produced his badge and saw it examined. The plainclothesman handed it back as though it had been a toy. "Now that you're here, what do you want?" he asked.

"First, suppose you tell me what the flap is. And what's your rank?"

"Sergeant. A suicide. From the looks of the body he jumped from a great height—near to the top. It happened about ten minutes ago."

Harbizon was fully alert and was aware that his heartbeat had picked up. "Who's the victim?" he asked sharply.

"We don't know yet; there's no ID on the body."

"Need any help?"

"No." With that the plainclothesman turned away.

Harbizon was about to go inside when he saw a bit of action that interested him—another man, obviously a policeman, was escorting a reluctant lobby attendant out of doors. The man had no rain protection, but that did not appear to matter. As Harbizon stood carefully still and watched, the attendant was taken over to where a form lay covered with a blanket on the sidewalk. He was made to bend down while a corner of the blanket was lifted.

Despite the darkness, and the rain, Harbizon saw the man react, jerking himself back as though from something unclean. He was quite elderly, and his thin body offered little in the way of physical stamina to support him. He covered his face with his hands as if to blot out the gruesome sight and then, with great reluctance, he spoke. "I think so," he stammered. "I can't be sure, the way he looks now, but yes, I think I know him."

At that moment, with the sure instinct that had guided him so many times, Harbizon's last doubt was removed. The odds against it being the man he had come to see were probably at least two hundred to one, considering the size of the building, but his man was about to be warned of a possible attempt on his life. And suicide was often the first guess in many homicides. Without ceremony he walked three brisk steps to where the attendant was standing and asked, "Is it Mr. Brown?"

The attendant looked up, grateful that he did not have to pronounce the name himself. "Yes," he said. "It's him."

Almost at once Harbizon was tapped on the shoulder. He turned to find a man he had not seen before, a large and impressive man who was in no mood to play games. "Come in here," he said with sharp authority and led the way into the lobby. As soon as they were both out of the rain he turned and confronted Harbizon. "How long have you known that man?" he asked, his voice quick and abrupt.

"I never met him. I talked to him on the phone about four hours ago."

"Who are you and what do you want?"

Once more Harbizon produced his credentials. "I've already advised your headquarters that I'm in your jurisdiction. I came here to see Brown, the man who jumped—if he did."

His interrogator picked that up immediately. "Do you doubt it's suicide?"

"At the moment, yes. I'd like to check one or two things about the body, if I may."

"All right, come outside." The speaker did not bother to introduce himself, but Harbizon overlooked it. It was a vile night for man or beast, and few people could remain courteous under such circumstances.

With a wave of his hand the big man cleared Harbizon to look at the corpse. He folded the blanket back and surveyed the body for a few seconds, noting that the deceased had been a sizable man. Since the body had struck face down, there was almost nothing left of the features. The hair at the crown of the head showed baldness enough to indicate an age of perhaps fifty. When he had noted all that, Harbizon bent down and carefully examined the dead man's shoes. He looked especially at the soles. The shoes were quite new and obviously expensive. They could even have been custom made.

"If you want to examine the shoe, take it off."

Harbizon accepted the invitation without looking up. He slipped the shoe off and then got to his feet. "I don't want to butt in here," he said, "but if I may, I'd like to see the place he came from."

Despite the continuing soaking rain, the man who

had been talking to him softened his attitude. "I don't see any harm in your giving us a hand if you'd like," he said. "Come on along."

Thoroughly wet to the point where his clothes clung to his skin, Harbizon went back into the lobby where his guide punched an elevator button. The doorman stood back, wanting to say something, but knowing that he had better not. It was his job to see that *no one* was admitted into the building until a tenant had requested it, but the police were another matter. He only hoped that they would finish quickly and then go away before too many people saw them. He also hoped fervently that the body outside had been removed, or would be within the next two or three minutes.

Harbizon pushed the button for the twenty-third floor which got an immediate reaction from the Chicago detective. "How did you know?" he asked.

"Brown told me. I made an appointment with him by telephone."

"For what time?"

"Nine-thirty this evening. I got here at nine-fourteen."

"You're pretty precise."

"My job."

"What's your field?"

"Major felonies. We have a small department. Before I signed on, I did homicide for eight years."

"No wonder."

When the door opened the Chicago man led the way down the hall to the proper door. He knocked sharply and waited briefly for an answer. When none came, he fitted the key that the desk clerk had given him into the lock and opened the door.

The apartment was a definition of luxury. Despite the streaming rain, Harbizon could see that in better weather it would command a spectacular view of both the lake and the Loop area. He estimated the rent at five thousand dollars a month unless it was one of those deals where you own your apartment outright. The carpeting was thick to the point of being Sybaritic, and the furniture was of top custom quality. Obviously, the late Mr. Brown had lived very well indeed.

There was a cunningly lighted bar at one end of the long living room. Harbizon went there immediately and looked carefully at the bare top. "Have one if you want to," his companion said. "He won't miss it."

Harbizon turned. "Suppose you had a bar stocked like that and you were about to jump over the railing and end your own life. What would you do?"

"I'd have a good stiff belt or two to brace myself. But he could have carried the glass somewhere else, even outside onto the balcony."

"Would he carefully put the liquor bottle back in place first?"

The Chicago detective stood stock still for a moment or two, then he nodded agreement. "You know your business," he conceded. "I'm glad you're here. I'm Lieutenant Hanratty, watch commander."

Harbizon offered a quick handshake and then deliberately fell behind as his companion walked toward the door that opened onto the terrace. There was a small throw rug dropped in front of it, possibly for use by the fastidious owner to wipe his feet before venturing back onto his sixty-dollar-a-square-yard carpeting.

Hanratty opened the door and let the wind come in. It blew quite strongly, but carried little water—the overhang of the terrace above offered some protection from the rain. On the terrace itself, which cantilevered out from the building like all the others, there were two or three pieces of aluminum patio furniture minus their covers. Surrounding them was a four-foot-high railing.

Harbizon took in the scene, then without asking permission he got down on his knees and gave full attention to the place where it was most likely that Brown had stood before taking his fatal plunge. He chose the spot directly in front of the doorway. A man about to kill himself would come out and go over, not walk around in the rain first. He had loved luxury—that was all too apparent—and even in his last moments he would not have subjected himself to the wretched weather.

After three or four minutes of the most careful examination he reached his conclusion. During the time that he had been occupied he had entirely ignored the rain, the wind that came with it, and the terrifying drop directly in front of his face. When he got to his feet, he stepped inside where Hanratty was patiently waiting for him to finish. "Well?" the watch commander asked.

"Call out your homicide boys," Harbizon answered. "I'm almost certain that it's murder."

10

For a few seconds Hanratty did nothing except stand still and look at his colleague—evaluating him. Then he spoke. "Give me a for instance."

Harbizon was ready for that. "Three things, to start with. The shoe. The absence of any scratches on the deck outside where he went over. And the misplaced throw rug."

Hanratty picked up the shoe, turned it over, and studied the sole. When he had done that he went to the telephone and called the homicide people. "I know that it's a foul night," he said, "but it looks like a killing. The victim was a big shot."

He hung up the instrument and turned to Harbizon. "Now what?" he asked.

"I'd like to talk to the doorman. Can you get him up here?"

A call on the house phone took care of that. Three minutes later the bedraggled doorman, his wet uniform hanging like a sack, came to the door. It was wide open and the owner of the apartment was dead, but he still knocked. Harbizon gestured him to come in without suggesting that an ordeal was to follow.

In response the doorman entered, cautiously, and waited to see what was wanted of him.

"Did Mr. Brown normally receive many visitors?" Harbizon asked.

"Some, sir. Not a great many."

"Of those appointments, from your observation would you say that they were mostly of a business kind?"

"I would think not, sir."

"I take it that Mr. Brown was not married."

"That's right, sir. He was divorced—three times."

"Did he tell you that?"

"No, sir, but it was common knowledge in the building. It has been in the papers."

"I see. Now, the man is dead, and nothing you might say can hurt him. Remembering that, was he in the habit of entertaining young women from time to time?"

The doorman hesitated a half second before he nodded. "We're not supposed to discuss the residents," he said, "but that's true."

"Any one young lady in particular?"

"I don't think so."

"All right, now pay very close attention to this. I called Mr. Brown earlier this evening and made an appointment to see him at nine-thirty."

"I know, sir, because Mr. Brown went out earlier and left word for you. He said that if you arrived before he got back, you were to wait in the lobby."

"Did he give you my name?"

"No, he just said that a gentleman would be calling. I assume he meant you, sir, because I saw you arrive by cab shortly after . . ."

"I understand." Harbizon turned to his Chicago colleague. "You see the point, of course. Brown definitely intended to see me. He gave me an appointment. If he had wanted to duck me, he wouldn't have left word for me to wait. He would have said that he wouldn't be back tonight at all."

He turned again to the doorman. "If a tenant doesn't want to see somebody, is it usual for you to say that he's out?"

The doorman bobbed his head. "We do it all the time. It's orders."

Hanratty picked it up. "I get it. If he was expecting you and wanted the meeting, he wouldn't pick that time to jump. But there's a hole in it. Suppose he learned something while he was out that made him decide to kill himself immediately. In that case, he could have hurried back here, braced himself with a couple of good strong belts, and gone over the railing."

"That's sound logic," Harbizon agreed, "but Brown agreed to see me only after I told him that his life might be in danger. That shook him. As of three hours ago, he very much wanted to live—enough to let me come and drip all over his expensive white carpeting."

Hanratty looked at the doorman. "This isn't the time to hold anything back," he said. "Do you know where Brown went tonight?"

The doorman didn't want to talk for the sake of his job, but he knew he had no choice. "I put him in a cab, and I heard him give the address."

"Did you recognize it?"

"I've heard it before."

"Give it to me."

Once more the doorman let his misery show, then he supplied the information. Harbizon went to the telephone, picked up an index that was beside it, and began to check the pages. Within a minute he found the entry he wanted. While Hanratty released the doorman, he dialed and waited for three rings until a feminine voice answered.

"This is Lieutenant Harbizon of the police department," he said with calm smoothness. "This is just a routine check. Are you Helen Heinemann?"

"Yes. What's happened?"

"We're simply verifying the movements of Mr. Irving Brown earlier this evening. Can you confirm that he paid you a visit?"

"Look, I don't want to get involved in anything!"

"You have nothing to worry about; all we want to affirm is that you saw Mr. Brown this evening."

"All right, he was here. But you can't prove we did anything we shouldn't."

"Miss Heinemann, I don't give a damn what you did, just answer one question. Did anything happen while Mr. Brown was with you to upset him? Did he receive any phone calls?"

"He didn't get any calls and there was nothing wrong with him. He left here happy. He always does. Ask him."

"Thank you, Miss Heinemann, you've been very helpful." He hung up. "Nothing shook up Brown while he was with the girl," he reported. "She let me get off the line without flooding me with questions. If she had been lying, she would have been a lot more curious."

The point made, he took a minute or two to go through the whole apartment. The kitchen was sparsely stocked, but what was on the shelves was gourmet food. The main bedroom was, as Harbizon had expected, almost wildly luxurious and exotically decorated. A lavish, life-sized nude, explicitly detailed, hung on one wall. He returned to the living room.

Hanratty went to the bar. "What'll you have?" he asked.

Harbizon was still wet and chilled. "Scotch and soda," he answered. "Whatever he's got that's good."

Hanratty was surveying the bottles. "You should see the stuff. Nothing but the best." He reached for a bottle. "You're getting twelve-year-old, will that do?" The Chicago detective filled two glasses with whiskey, ice, and soda, then passed one of them to Harbizon. "It's a helluva night," he commented.

As they clinked glasses, sounds in the corridor announced the arrival of the homicide team. The four additional men who came into the room didn't crowd it in the least. While his colleague began to set up more drinks on the bar, Harbizon briefed the investigators despite the fact that he was not in his own jurisdiction. "About the shoe," he concluded, "a check of the sole by eyesight alone showed some tiny particles pressed into the leather. It was wet, of course, and that may have softened the leather a little. If Brown had deliberately jumped to his death, he would either have had to climb over the railing or else take a kind of running leap. In either case there would be some traces on the concrete deck—it's freshly painted. There's nothing there. I checked it carefully.

"Something else," he continued. "There's a small throw rug by the door to the terrace. The rug belongs in the bedroom. I can show you the spot."

He was interrupted by a question. "You mean, someone put the rug out there, got him to stand on it, and then yanked it away?"

"Something like that. Obviously, I don't know how it was done—not yet. But if you check, you'll see that the rug is wet."

"But that doesn't make sense! If Brown was supposed to have jumped by himself, why try to prevent any scratches on the terrace?"

"I didn't say that the idea was to conceal any marks, only that the absence of marks indicated that a rug was used. Brown certainly didn't do it himself."

Another of the homicide men spoke up. "Don't you agree that, on principle, he'd be very conscious of that relatively low railing and the wet deck on a night like tonight?"

"Yes, but remember that he lived here and presumably was out on that terrace a good bit of the time. He was familiar with it and any vertigo would have worn off."

Hanratty stated the obvious. "We'll have to check the whole building for guests and any tenants who might have had it in for Brown. And there must be two hundred apartments."

As Harbizon was allowing himself to be grateful that that wouldn't be his job, Hanratty touched him on the shoulder. "I'll fix you another drink," he offered, "then I want to talk to you."

They went into the huge bedroom, taking their glasses with them, and sat down on luxurious wool chairs so soft that they seemed to have no frames. "There're a few things you haven't told me yet," the Chicago detective began. "First, what's your connection with Brown? Why did you tell him his life was in danger? And why are you so far away from your own jurisdiction?" His tone was casual, but that didn't dilute the firmness of his questions. Obviously he wanted answers.

Harbizon tasted his drink without a pang of conscience and then took it from the top. He described the first homicide that had brought him into the case and added as much information as was necessary to bring Hanratty fully up to speed on the stock market killings.

"Since I didn't have any leads to work on, I checked to see who might be next on the list," he concluded. "Three different people suggested

Brown as a likely candidate. I was going to warn him, then ask if we could get together to have him covered—the time seemed about right. He died a few minutes before I got here."

"Do you think it all ties in?"

"I'd like to look through his papers if I may. The second bedroom is fitted out as a study, and there's a big desk in there."

"Go ahead. Officially, you're cooperating with us."

"No other way," Harbizon agreed.

The blustering rain had quieted to a slow drizzle, and a lead-gray dawn was struggling to take over when he finished. During the long night Harbizon's eyes had grown heavy and then had smarted painfully, but he had kept on with his work. He found a private account book of records that was kept in a very simple code. In a matter of minutes he worked that out, and the figures were revealed before him. As he read and studied them, he had to fight with himself to keep from becoming emotionally involved. The chicanery was blatant, as the week-to-week records revealed. The market letter that Brown had published had been a cunning device to support his own ends to a degree Harbizon could hardly believe. And running through for the past four months there had been a steady thread that dealt with Sphinx Wire and Cable. Then, at a little after six, he found the letter marked TOTALLY CONFIDENTIAL in a double envelope that had come to Brown from Nathan Lockheim. It was absolute proof that any jury would have accepted at full value, but it was worthless except for possible civil actions since both men were dead.

When he went back into the huge living room, the homicide crew had left. Hanratty was asleep in one of the massive chairs. He had his head thrown back, his mouth open, and he was softly snoring. As Harbizon looked at him he knew that it was part of the life of a cop—a constant, endless process of slogging work without regard to normal hours, murderous overtime, and precious little thanks of any kind. He wondered for a moment why he had chosen this life for himself; then he wiped that thought away, as he had so often before, with the statement to himself that it was his profession. Without the police department, any major city in the nation could be reduced to an area of total disaster in thirty days. He wondered what kind of a family Hanratty had and whether they had any home life at all.

He shook his colleague awake and said, "Let's get out of here."

Outside the morning air held no encouragement—there was less rain, but that was all. Harbizon carried a large manila envelope with certain of Brown's documents in it. Hanratty woke up his rain-soaked car, coaxed it into unwilling life, and drove to an all-night restaurant that was a standard code-seven stop. Eggs, sausage, toast, and hot coffee helped to make the day seem a little brighter, and because he had a liberal expense account, Harbizon insisted on picking up the check. Both men were unshaven and utterly weary, but Harbizon turned down the idea of a hotel. Instead, he asked to be dropped off where he could catch the airport bus. Hanratty offered to take him all the way north to the terminal, but Harbizon refused. Somehow he rode back to the field, checked in with the airline that had the next flight to New York without caring which one it was, and went through the boarding gate into the waiting 727. He slept fitfully all the way to Kennedy Airport and thereby got a little uncertain rest.

Forgetting the expense for once, he took a cab to Boylesport and his own waiting bed. As he rode, despite his acute fatigue, something was nagging in his brain. He tried to bring it forward into his consciousness, but he couldn't do so. Tantalizingly it told him that there was something he had missed back in that high-rise, luxury apartment in Chicago. Something he should have seen and grasped when it had been right in front of him.

He tried to think about it, but his overladen mind refused to oblige. It reminded him again, sharply, of the utter desirability of his own bed, of cool, clean sheets, and of undisturbed rest.

When he got home he did not even take time to read the accumulated mail. He got out of his clothes, washed, and then climbed into bed at close to noon, utterly exhausted. His last waking thought, which barely had time to catch him still conscious, was that there was *something*, plain and apparent, that he had missed.

He awoke somewhere in the middle of the night, his body aching and with the beginning of a cold. He got into a bathrobe and made himself something to eat. As soon as he had the food inside his stomach he drew a hot bath and soaked in the tub until all of the stiffness had gone and he felt fully relaxed. He toweled down carefully, went back into the bedroom, and climbed back between the sheets, planning just to lie there and think. But the bed was too warm and too soft for that. He went to sleep once more and didn't wake again until the very early dawn.

There was nothing important in his mail, but he was sure that there would be messages at his office. After he had shaved and dressed he went in, arriving while the thin graveyard shift was still on duty. As he had expected, there were a number of messages, some of them casual and others of prime interest. It was too early to place any calls, but he was rested now and ready to charge in against whatever obstacles he might find in his path. Part of his energy came from the fact that he had found a possible new angle to the case.

When at last it was eight-thirty he put in a call to Charles Dietrich who had phoned twice while he had been out of town. "I'm back," he reported simply. "What have you got?"

Dietrich was all business. "First, I had a nice long talk with Harold Horowitz, the boyfriend of the Chinese girl. He's a slippery bastard, totally self-centered, and very much money-oriented. He admitted that he tried to package his girlfriend as a super call girl and still can't understand why she refused all that loot. Anyhow, he finally gave me an account of his movements on the night that San Marco was done in. He had had a tiff with the Chow girl, so he had gone off tomcatting to see what else he could find. He ran a girl down in a bar, and she provided his entertainment for the evening."

"Have you been able to locate her?"

"No problem. She's a professional working girl known to the precinct vice boys where she operates. She passes on some very useful information from time to time, so they leave her relatively alone. She fully confirmed her evening with Horowitz and supplied an interesting detail to prove it."

"Such as?"

"When he was circumcised the job was botched. She described it in detail. I've established that she was right."

"There could have been another occasion."

"I did think of that, John; I wasn't born yesterday. The bartender who made the arrangements was cooperative and confirmed the fact that Horowitz was in the bar for some time. So I don't think Horowitz is guilty, and even if he is, there's no hope of a conviction."

"How about the Chinese girl herself?" Harbizon asked. "Have you talked to her?"

"Yes, I have. I discovered that there are inner depths to you, my friend. She spoke of you in quite complimentary terms. Something about being a gentleman. I didn't get quite all of it, because I had other matters on my mind. If the Churchill girl is to be believed, it was a man who shot San Marco, so the field is narrowed down a little."

"Go on," Harbizon invited.

"I went to see Elliott of the NYPD. The Korngold case has been closed. They're satisfied that it was a bona fide traffic accident despite the fact that the Korngold killing touched off a major reaction against stock market manipulators and the like. The driver involved, a guy named Abe Schwartz, was nailed for felony hit and run. He's off the street and has a trial coming up. He was unlucky. He was picked up in his own car for a minor traffic violation. He made such a case of it, the officers involved considered it probable cause and shook down his car. He was running a small load of heroin, about sixty balloons packed for street sale."

"I take it he's inside."

"Warm and dry. He hasn't a prayer of beating the rap since the probable cause is OK. The charge is possession for sale, and since he was on bail at the time, he's looking at about three years."

"Anything new on Forrester?"

"Yes, but not to be discussed over the phone. It seems he has some friends."

"Mutual friends?"

"You could put it that way."

"We'd better talk about that."

"I want to. Which reminds me, Ted Walchewski of the NYPD wants to see us both ASAP. Can you come in?"

Harbizon made an appointment for just after lunch and then turned his attention to the accumulated paperwork that was on his desk. He cleared it away and then headed for the city. He had a new angle, and he wanted to explore it without any more delay.

He went first to the newspaper office where he hoped to find either Gene Burroughs or Bert Schneider in. He could have made an appointment, but he had his reasons for not doing that. Luck was with him; both of the columnists were in and what was more, they seemed glad to see him. "Have you got anything for us?" Schneider asked.

Harbizon looked around for a moment. The two reporters had taken him to a vacant corner office that was stark, cluttered, and partitioned by clear glass that didn't reach all the way up to the ceiling. It was a private sanctuary only by courtesy. It was more like a half-filled goldfish bowl. "Maybe I do," he answered. "I've been on the Coast and in Chicago."

"We know about Chicago," Schneider told him. "We get the first info off the AP wire. How did you happen to be there at exactly that time?"

"I've been asking myself the same question," Harbizon answered. "One possibility is that the man went over the railing rather than see me, but that's hard to accept."

"Wipe it off," Burroughs advised. "No way. If he didn't want to see you, badge or not he could have kept you out. Unless you went and got a warrant.

The tenants of those expensive high rises pay for protection, and they get it."

"How much of the story have you got?" Harbizon asked.

"A lot," Burroughs answered. "Irving Brown jumped from the terrace of his apartment shortly after nine at night. It was raining heavily, but despite that it's hard to believe that he slipped."

"For one thing," Schneider added, "people don't go out on open terraces in that kind of weather. Anyhow, he jumped. But, get this, sometime later the homicide people were called in, on a suicide. You're a cop; what do you make of that?"

"Suspicious circumstances," Harbizon answered promptly. "A suicide is always subject to suspicion unless there are several things that point to it. Known difficulties, a note, two or three other things. In this case Brown wasn't known to have any reason to kill himself, and off the record, no note was left."

"And that was enough to trigger a homicide investigation."

"There were some other things, but I didn't come here to talk about the Brown death in Chicago. I've got a new angle. Can I discuss it strictly off the record?"

"Off the record," Schneider answered promptly. "You ought to know, we've never broken that commitment."

"Then here it is. Of the four known victims, not counting the traffic casualty, three have turned out to be heavy womanizers. The guy in Los Angeles was living with one woman and screwing several others on the side. Brown, in Chicago, regularly entertained young women in his apartment at night."

"How about Lockheim?" Burroughs asked.

"That's why I'm here," Harbizon replied. "I know that he did have a regular girlfriend, and having met his wife, I sympathize with that completely. But was that all? I'd like to know if Nathan Lockheim had sexual activity other than his regular mistress and to what extent."

"You see an irate husband or lover?" Schneider asked.

"I didn't say that, but it could be that someone objects to the victims' stock market activity *and* moral character. There are a lot of crackpots, and some not so cracked who have strong views. Or, sometimes there is someone who has been sexually deprived and who 'gets even' by taking out those who have more than their share."

Schneider was thinking. "Look," he said, "that might just hold water. The last thing San Marco heard, just before he was shot, was his assassin saying something like, 'that's the last time you'll screw anybody.' That could be taken literally."

"We know about it," Burroughs explained, "because we read the police report. You know the policy on that."

Harbizon nodded. "We let the press read our reports, too, if there isn't anything in them that's confidential. Now, if you guys want to help me, see what you can dig up on Nathan Lockheim's sex life. If you hit anything juicy, let me know. Thousands got badly stung on Sphinx Wire and Cable, but if we're looking for a prude or a fanatic as well, it might help a lot."

"Count on us," Burroughs said. "If there's anything to be found out, we'll get it. If we do and it jells, then we get the story—agreed?"

"Agreed," Harbizon said.

Lieutenant Walchewski looked like a quarterback who had just completed a forty-four-yard touchdown pass to take the lead in the scoring. He had seen action and he was thirsting for more. Dietrich was already in his office when Harbizon arrived. Walchewski picked up his phone and passed the word to Sergeant Elliott that the meeting was about to begin. Two minutes later Elliott came in, brushing his hair back, although for once it did not need it.

Because it was his office, and because he was charged up for the conference, Walchewski took the floor. "As of this moment we have five men dead who've been up to their necks in white-collar crime. Some of it may have been technically within the law, but it was crime just the same. Don't quote me, for God's sake, but these deaths have triggered a reform movement that's the best thing that has happened for years. Whoever has been knocking these guys over has done a major service for his country. That doesn't mean that I condone it, but the facts are there. Are you all up on what's been happening?"

Harbizon shook his head; so did Dietrich. "All right," Walchewski continued, "let me give you a fast once-over. You know about the commodity trading markets. As far as I'm concerned they're pure gambling—people buying and selling things they have no use for and never expect to take delivery on. They bet against each other, which is their funeral except for the fact that it raises hob with food prices, farm income, and a lot of other damn important things. Well, the Commodity Trading Commission has suddenly gotten tough. The old argument that all the speculating created a stable market place has gone down the tube. There's a bill being prepared in Washington that will outlaw all speculative trading in commodity futures. If it passes, the only people who will be allowed to buy and sell are those who have a legitimate interest in the commodities they are dealing in. From now on, the speculators can bet on the horse races instead."

Harbizon drew a deep breath and let it out, but he did not comment.

"Up until now," Walchewski went on, "most of the major brokerage firms have been openly advertising tax shelters, which is a helluva note if you ask me. Schemes and devices to get around paying the taxes that the rest of us all face. Anyhow, there are about six bills pending in the congressional hopper to wipe out these shelters and to make it illegal to advertise ways and means of beating the Internal Revenue Service. The upper income brackets are screaming, but the public is getting more aroused every day, and that's a force no special privilege group can stop. Nixon found that out."

Walchewski picked up an out-of-town paper off his desk that had been folded open at the editorial page. "Listen to this," he said. "The editorial is called 'Justifiable Homicide?' It starts out by saying that there is such a thing in law: circumstances that excuse homicide. Then it goes on to say that while these Wall Street killings can't be condoned per se, they have brought about a long overdue reform movement that has great momentum, coast to coast. And that out of these illegal acts, it can't be denied that a great deal of good has come."

"I've got one for you," Dietrich cut in. "I haven't even told John about this yet. I haven't had a chance. Lockheim's widow has been hit with a massive class action lawsuit. I don't know how valid it is, but Sphinx Wire and Cable is a party to it. And, since they're a government supplier, the Justice Department just might get involved. It all has some fascinating possibilities."

"Some lawyers are going to make out, that's for sure," Elliott said. "I'm only sitting in because our finding that the Korngold death was accidental is being challenged. They don't have a prayer, but apparently he was some kind of an operator."

"His estate's been attached," Walchewski said. "The government is interested because it seems that he was using a tax shelter that isn't valid. At least Internal Revenue is going after it full bore."

"How about the San Marco estate?" Harbizon asked.

"So far there's no action there, but the clean-up wave is gaining by the hour, and a lot of floor traders are suddenly getting religion."

"It's a field day for Burroughs and Schneider," Dietrich said.

Walchewski made his chair creak under him. "Hell yes! They've got enough stuff right now to keep their column going for months ahead. They were sniping at the market and getting nowhere when this all started. Believe me, the New York Stock Exchange and the other market places have their defenses. But when Korngold, in particular, died, what was uncovered then was enough to turn the whole thing around. Now the NYSE is changing its rules, making them a lot tougher. They may even ban margin trading and option sales. It will bust the brokerage houses, but the public could be millions ahead."

"The brokerage houses have a legitimate function," Harbizon said. "At least it seems that way to me at the moment. But there is obviously a lot that needs fixing."

"There's one key bill," Walchewski said. "If it passes, the brokerage houses will have to follow the clients' instructions as to the type of stocks they recommend and offer. An investment client, for example, that's registered that way, can't be sold a speculative or volatile stock unless he first signs a waiver stating that he knows that the stock in question isn't investment quality. Then the monkey is on his back. You guys aren't involved with the market, so the technical details won't mean a lot, but it boils down to the fact that the stock and commodity markets are through as national gambling halls, the way things are going now. The widows and orphans are going to be protected for a change, as well as some of the rest of us who try to put something by whenever we can."

"But you can't just go out and knock off people because they are sharpies and manipulators," Harbizon said.

"Of course not," Walchewski agreed. "I said that it can't be condoned, but how would you feel if someone had succeeded in shooting Hitler early in the game? It would have been murder, but I'd like to sit on the jury that tried the man who did it."

"What we're talking about is the judicial process," Harbizon said. "Thank God we're not part of that game. I once spent seven months, off and on, and finally nailed a child molester that was an animal. I went to court with an air-tight case and a confession. He got off because he claimed that he hadn't understood his rights because they weren't read to him in Spanish."

Dietrich calmed him down. "We've all had cases like that," he said. "You don't have to tell us about it. But the killings have got to stop. Either that or admit that we no longer live in a civilized society."

"We'll stop them," Harbizon promised. "At the moment I don't know how, but I promise you it will be done. Wait and see."

11

As he paused a moment before he pushed the bell, John Harbizon asked himself, almost savagely, if he was behaving like a damn fool. By her own admission Helen Chow had been the bought and paid for mistress of William San Marco, and her touching story about having done it in order to get back money that was owed to her family was just a little hard to believe. She had the looks, the youth, the polish, and the other ingredients necessary to be a first-class, high-priced call girl. Ruthlessly he told himself that he was a middle-aged policeman with nothing whatever that would attract such a girl to him, professional or not. Therefore, it had to be something else—something she wanted.

He rang the bell and waited. She had invited him, she wanted something, and if he handled things the right way, he might end up with some vital information concerning his case. Miss Helen Chow knew more than she had told.

When she opened the door and he saw her, his hard resolution fled. She had on a simple black dress with a white scarf around her throat that set off her black hair. Her skirt flared just a little in a way that emphasized her femininity. A silver-and-turquoise Navajo ornament was pinned below her left shoulder. "Good evening," she said. "I'm glad you could come."

The first hard thought that hit Harbizon was that he could not have any part of the very high-quality merchandise that was on display. Women like that were reserved for the very handsome and gifted, for the very wealthy, and, in most cases, for a combination of the two. For reasons of her own she was allowing him a little of her company. The reason would emerge later.

Harbizon came in, aware that he was trespassing. "Thank you for asking me," was the best he could manage.

"Please sit down, lieutenant, and let me fix you a drink."

"Since this is a purely social occasion," he said, "I suggest we drop the title. My name is Harbizon, or John if you would like."

"What would you like, John? I have scotch, bourbon, vodka, gin, and white wine."

"A scotch and Seven."

"Coming up."

She disappeared for a few moments, and when she came back she had two glasses in her hands. When she gave Harbizon his, he touched her slender, tapered fingers and felt an immediate reaction to that limited physical contact. He sat down on the sofa with her, but at the opposite end so that there was a space of several feet between them. He tasted his drink and found it, as he had expected, excellent.

For a few seconds he felt awkward. He was no good at small talk, and he was embarrassingly aware of it. His hostess seemed to understand that and spoke in such a quiet way that answering her was no strain at all. Within a few minutes his hesitation had been broken down, and he was much more comfortable. He had resolved before he came that he would not discuss police business in any way unless she brought it up or else gave him an opening he could not pass by. To his amazement, before he found the bottom of his first glass he was telling her the bare bones of his marriage and why it had broken up so disastrously.

"It wasn't Gwen's fault," he explained. "It was mine—and the kind of work I do. I was a sergeant then in a big city department, which meant that the pressures were constant. Sometimes I was gone from the house for two or three days, and she had no idea where I was or what I was doing. She had every right to be worried, and upset. Gradually it just got worse until we both knew that it was no go any longer."

"Where is she now?"

"Living in St. Louis, I think. I'm not sure."

Helen Chow refilled his glass, then she went out into the kitchen of her apartment. She had already set a small table for two in her living room a little way back from the windows. It gleamed with white linen and shining silverware. He could not remember when anyone had set a table like that for him. As if to underline his thought, Helen came back in with a bottle of wine in her hands. She poured out two glasses and then put the bottle in a holder that was waiting to receive it. "Do you have any eating taboos?" she asked.

Harbizon shook his head. "None at all. I'll like whatever you have."

She smiled her appreciation of that, left, and came back with a tureen she put on the table. "To start," she said, "I have birds' nest soup. It really is made from birds' nests, but it's thoroughly purified in the cooking, and we consider it a delicacy. I hope you will like it."

He sat down after putting her into her chair, laid his napkin on his lap, and then tried the soup. He put completely out of his mind what it was and thought of it only as the start of his dinner. The first taste told him that it was delicious. He was much closer to Helen Chow now, and her proximity, touching distance away, had a decided effect on him. But he could not dismiss the idea that she was treating him this well because she wanted something from him—something important to her.

Then she began talking with him again, and once more he found that he could respond easily. She mentioned literature and music, sounding him out as to his own interests. He had the feeling that this disturbing young woman could see directly through him and knew without asking which subjects he liked and how much he knew about them.

The main course she offered him was duck stuffed with some kind of tantalizing filling. He had no idea what the dish was, he had never had it before, but it was clearly something special.

"Did you make this yourself?" he asked.

"Yes, I did," she answered. "I like to cook, I enjoy good food, and I hope you're impressed."

"I am—very much."

"I believe that it's very important a man think of a girl as a good cook. It could carry a lot of weight." Her mouth quirked a little as she said that, and he knew that she was playing with him—she knew her own beauty and her appeal, and she knew too that he was a plain-faced man with no special virtues and certainly no brilliant future. He would never be able to provide mounds of money, social glamour, and the kind of jet-set living that her superior assets could capture for her. She wouldn't always be this beautiful, but Oriental women, he knew, hung onto it longer than anyone else. She would be a knockout when she was fifty—and beyond.

"You are a fine cook," he said. "And a brilliant conversationalist. I'm enjoying my evening very much."

"I'm so glad." She said it as if she meant it. Later they moved back to the davenport where she provided tiny thin glasses of an after-dinner liqueur. Harbizon sat as he had before, half facing her and at one end of the sofa. He wished, for a moment or two, that he might have been born into a situation where he could live like this every day. It wasn't his lot, but he allowed himself a very brief dream.

"What else do you do besides cook, design, and all of the other things we talked about?" he asked.

"I'll tell you later," she promised. "Right now, there are all sorts of interesting things I want to ask you. Have you ever been to the Far East?"

Harbizon lost track of the time. All that he knew was that he was having an evening completely apart from his work—an evening free of abrupt telephone calls, sudden disasters, and the other hazards of his profession. He allowed himself to imagine that he was entitled to the kind of life she typified and talked of things that he would never dare to mention to his colleagues on the police force. He had read quite a bit, and it seemed that every worthwhile thing he had picked up somehow came into the conversation.

He had another liqueur or two—he didn't bother to keep count—and he knew that his inhibitions were considerably softened, but still he managed to satisfy himself just by conversation. He had ceased to wonder why she had invited him; he concentrated instead on being the best possible guest. For a little while he allowed himself to think that this kind of woman was his just due, that he was equal to any man who might compete for her attention. Subconsciously, he knew it wasn't true, but he played the game and found that it came more easily than he could have hoped.

When he knew that it was close to the time when he would have to get up and break the spell by leaving, he returned without knowing why to the question he had asked her almost two hours before. "What else do you do?" he repeated. "I really want to know."

She looked down at her lap and ran an ivory white hand across her skirt before she looked up. "Sometimes, John, I read minds."

"In what way?"

She looked at him face to face, their eyes meeting as she spoke. "Shall I tell you what you have been thinking these last few minutes?"

"Yes, please."

As he spoke, he hoped to heaven that she couldn't do it. His private thoughts were his own, and he didn't want her to know them.

"Very well. I caught something in your manner. You looked at me for a moment and then there was pain on your face. Not a lot, but a little. You clasped your hands together and forced them down between your knees, as though you were trying to push a thought away. You were thinking, I believe, that I had once granted some privileges to William San Marco, and you were wondering why that man, with all of his flaws of character, achieved something that you can't have. Am I right?"

He drew a tight breath and held it for a second or so. She had come so close to the mark he did not dare to deny it. Since it was true, he gave the simplest answer he could. "Yes," he admitted.

"John, I want to tell you something. All men—all normal men—look at girls and think about them as sexual partners. It's the most natural thing in the world. Some men achieve a good many of their ambitions in that direction. A lot of them are crude, overbearing, and demanding. They think it's being forceful. You, John, are a fine and decent man, a gentleman. Consequently, you don't attack girls by trying to seduce them regardless of anything else. It's always been that way. The decent honorable types behave themselves and they don't make the grade. They won't push and fight or hand out a line of pure bullshit in order to get what they're after. And excuse my using that word, but there isn't any other. Men like you look for sex only from their wives. If they don't have a wife, they go without."

"Just suppose," Harbizon said, "that I had laid a strong campaign for you after dinner. Suppose I had forced myself on you, and played the part of the mean, hard man who wouldn't be denied. The kind they are using to illustrate the cigarette ads at the moment. Would I have gotten you into the bedroom?"

She looked at him. "Possibly—if I wanted it that way. Not otherwise. But the question is academic, because if you were that way, I wouldn't have invited you here. I never cooked a dinner for San Marco. I made him take me out. He asked me to prepare a meal for him once. I gave him hot dogs and canned beans."

The thought of that took a little of the bitterness away. It was all so near, but actually so far because she was right. He would never force anything; it wasn't the way he wanted to live his life.

He stood up and faced her. "I have a long way to go," he said. "I've had a wonderful evening."

Helen Chow stood up and came toward him. Without ceremony she put an arm across his shoulders and lifted her face toward him.

He knew that he was expected to kiss her, but he knew also that she would turn her head quickly and present him with her cheek. So many women did that. As he drew her to him, actually touching her for the first time, a kind of fire seemed to run through his fingers. It was far from the first time that he had taken hold of a woman other than his wife, but none of his previous experiences pertained this time. It was utterly different.

And she did not turn her head away from him; she tilted it just a little and pressed her lips on his. Her body was beside his and his whole being responded. He was careful not to kiss her too hard, but he was not gentle. He broke the contact for a moment, looked at her, and then came back for more. At that moment he didn't give a damn for the case, what she might know, or anything else. He had not had a woman that close to him in too long a time, and never one so utterly appealing.

He did not know how long it lasted; he was on some plane suspended at an unknown point in space where ordinary consideration did not apply. It could have been a minute, two minutes, or as much as five. The thing that encompassed him was the fact that she was not simply giving him a good-night kiss. She seemed to welcome the contact between them, for reasons that God only knew. At last he recovered himself and stood, still very close to her, but with his arms at his sides.

She looked at him evenly and openly, an intelligent young woman talking to a mature and capable man. "You're welcome to stay if you'd like," she said.

As soon as she had left him and had gone into the little dressing room, he had washed and stolen a little of the mouthwash that he found in the bathroom. After that he had gotten out of his clothes quickly and had climbed into her bed with a strong sense of unreality. He had seen her carefully lock and bolt the only door, but he could not dismiss concern from his mind. It could be some kind of a trap. Then he came to his senses. He was about to go to bed with a damn good-looking woman, and that wasn't even a misdemeanor anymore.

She had set the light in the bedroom very low, but it was enough. When she came out of her dressing room she was a milk-and-ivory goddess. He watched her as she came toward him, bent down, and folded her side of the covers back. Then she was in bed beside him. He took her into his arms and from that moment every second of delay was a precious agony. He kissed her softly several times while he ran his free hand gently down her back, then he pressed her to him, cupping his hand to fit the shape of her soft buttock.

Never in his lifetime had he resorted to a professional, but he knew at once that while she was experienced, she would never be in that category. Her teeth stung his earlobe slightly, and her fingernails found his back. He buried his face in her neck, his lips against her warm flesh. For a few moments her face was above his, her exquisite features framed by her loosened hair. Then he rolled over, parted her legs, and was engulfed by ecstasy.

When he awoke he was lying on his back. His left arm was at his side; his right arm was outstretched and pillowing the head of Helen Chow. He became aware of daylight in the room; otherwise the hour was meaningless. He turned his head then and saw her face looking into his own. He was most conscious of her eyes—large, very dark, and limpid. Her lips formed a very slight quirk, more a silent communication than a smile.

John Harbizon was aware of several things at once—his hair was unruly, his face had to be covered with stubble, and his breath, in all probability, was not at its best. He looked at her again and the same eyes were looking back at him, silently, apparently approvingly, and intimately. It was then that he became fully aware that her body was still close to his and with a warmth for which there is no substitute.

"Good morning," she said.

He turned his body a little. "Have you been awake long?"

"No. I awoke just now. How do you feel?"

"I can't tell you," he answered, "because I never

felt like this before."

"Even when you were married?"

He didn't want to say an unkind thing about the girl who had shared a few years of his life, but he couldn't think of any evasion that would work. "No," he said, "not even then."

"I'll be back in a minute," she told him and then the warm bed was suddenly terribly empty. When she returned he got to his feet and went into the bathroom, still not knowing what time it was—or caring. He used the mouthwash again and hoped that it would be effective. He was conscious of looking his worst and would have given a great deal for a shower. Then he remembered what awaited him and the same feeling of disbelief came surging up once more.

But she was there, the upper sheet covering only part of her bare shoulders. "I used your mouthwash," he confessed.

"In the cabinet there's an electric razor," Helen said. "Before you jump to conclusions, it's brand new."

"Then how do you happen to have it?"

"I bought it for you."

That was the answer he had dared to hope for. He got back into bed, gathered her once more into his arms, but was content for the moment just to hold her that way. He kissed her quietly and gently, just to be sure that he could, and liked it so much that he did it twice more, asserting himself. Then he ran his fingers through her hair, admiring the texture of it and its shining blackness. "I want to know something," he said. "It's very important. I think you could have any man you ever wanted, discounting those in holy orders, so why did you ever allow— choose me? I don't possibly deserve it."

She kissed him effortlessly, making it a simple caress, more to please herself than him. "But you do," she answered. "And I'll tell you why."

She snuggled her head against his shoulder, making herself comfortable. "I told you about Harold's plan—how I was to become a very costly and exotic call girl. And how he and his uncle were going to invest my earnings for us to get married on. I came home that evening alone, and sat here thinking. One of the questions I asked myself was this: Of all of the men I have ever met, which one would be the least likely to offer me that kind of proposition. Several different people I knew ran through my mind, and then I came to you. There wasn't any doubt. You were the one . . . the exact opposite of the man who wanted to package me and sell me like merchandise. So I thought about you."

She stopped and looked at him again. Even in the early morning light, unwashed and without make-up, she had not lost an iota of her beauty.

"So you invited me to dinner," Harbizon said, speaking quietly toward the ceiling, "prepared a fabulous meal, and laid in a brand new electric razor."

"That was a gamble," she answered. "Not a very big one. I didn't know whether I would invite you to stay or not. I wanted to know you better first. I'm not a call girl, you know. I think you may have had the idea that I was—because of the way we met. I'm not, and I never will be."

She paused, but Harbizon was acutely careful to say nothing. She read him too well.

"I'm a designer—remember?" she went on. "I make a good salary, much better than you might think. And I pay my own rent. To an uncle of mine. He owns this building."

The kiss he gave her then lasted longer. In his heart he had the feeling that this would never happen to him again, therefore he was making the most of it during the one chance that he had.

"I believe in sex," she said. "I think it's one of the great blessings we have. Adults, like ourselves, should be free to enjoy it, properly, without any censure from anybody."

"That's quite a declaration," Harbizon said.

She traced a finger across his chest. "I didn't want to sound formal. What I meant was, no obligations—either way. Some girls can only see sex as part of love and marriage. I see it as part of living."

"How about in the morning?" he asked her.

"Good!" she breathed. "Before I cook your breakfast."

On the way back to Boylesport Harbizon tried to reassess himself and the fixed boundaries of his life. He had no intention whatever of changing his profession, but he allowed himself to relive in his mind the past fifteen hours and lock them permanently in his memory. Even their lighthearted conversation at breakfast, while he had eaten the bacon and eggs that she had so skillfully prepared.

"I suppose you've heard that ugly rumor about Chinese women," she had chided him.

"With utmost disbelief."

"Well, now you know it isn't so, don't you."

"Yes, I do, but I'd like to be reassured from time to time."

She had smiled at that, but she had said nothing in reply.

He was glad that he had stopped at a florist shop and had ordered something sent to her.

As the train took him closer and closer to his base of operation, the case that had been engaging his full attention forced itself back into his mind. That was as it should be. The famous gallants of old went out and slew dragons furiously during the daytime. Then after a rousing meal and a little practice swordplay, they would dispose of doublet and hose and make their women happy far, far into the night. They didn't have dental anesthetics in those days, but they knew how to live.

The scenery outside the window was so totally familiar he did not see it at all. Instead he was standing, mentally, in the middle of a huge, luxurious living room on a pouring night in Chicago, seeing something that he could not recall—something that danced maddeningly at the very edge of his memory. To capture it he went back to the first moment when the cab he had been in had pulled up before the high-rise building, after he had cleared the police line that had been hastily thrown up in the foul weather.

Patiently he retraced every minute—everything that he had seen or done, every word that had been spoken, every tiny thing he had noted. He missed it the first time through and he knew it; somewhere he had inadvertently skipped something. Once more he brought back the rain, the wet, jouncing cab, the policeman who had stopped him and had let him through only after he had identified himself.

The entrance to the building, the still drenching rain, the plainclothesman in the plastic raincoat who had challenged him, the reluctant doorman who had been taken out to see the body. The squashed thing that had been a man, the shoe he had taken off . . .

The body.

Something about the body.

He knew now where the thing was hiding, but he still didn't have it in his conscious mind.

Then it came. The body. The remains of a big burly man crushed horribly from a fall that had been something like two hundred and fifty feet through the sopping wet night, through the blackness, without a scream that had been heard; a plunge of several seconds that had ended with the instant transformation of a healthy, muscular man into a squashed corpse that had been dreadful to look at. It had not been easy to take off that shoe, even though he had kept his eyes away from the main part of the body while he was untying it.

He returned to his office with a whole new channel of investigation opened to him. He had a great many things to do, and he would have to be extremely careful not to let his own foot slip. One mistake now and the whole thing would be forever out of his reach.

12

After he had cleared the top of his desk and had picked up his routine for the day, Harbizon went to see the chief. There was little protocol in the Boylesport Police Department. He just picked a free moment to walk in and sit down, knowing that he would be welcome. He exchanged a few of the usual agreeable remarks and then came to the point. "I'm not making any promises whatever," he said, "but I may have found the end of the tunnel in the Lockheim killing. I believe that I know who did it—and why."

The chief did not let it show too much, but he was close to elated. "John, that's wonderful! I don't know how in the world you did it, but accept my congratulations. You are certainly a major asset to this department."

"Thank you, but I haven't earned all that yet."

"I'm sure you will. What are the chances for arrest and conviction?"

Harbizon shook his head. "It may not be possible. If everything works out, we'll be able to report in due time that the case has been solved, but owing to circumstances we can't reveal, the guilty party may not be brought to trial."

"Do you think the citizenry will buy that?"

"If we put it the right way, yes. We might leak it out that a suicide was involved. That almost always closes a matter."

The chief thought for a few moments while his lips unconsciously reflected his thoughts. "Nat Lockheim was not a popular man. He belonged to the yacht club and all that, but few people actually cared for him. I'm inclined to think that the suicide idea will satisfy almost everyone. Discretion is very much appreciated in this community."

Harbizon was grateful for that. The attitude of the chief, and that of the whole department, was one of the reasons why he was contented to remain with a very small organization where major crimes were not often encountered. It was a gentlemanly police force that knew how to do its job, but kept its cuffs clean in the process. There was a lot to recommend that approach whenever the community being served made it possible. On Manhattan Island it would have been out of the question.

"Tell me," the chief continued. "That man who jumped to his death in Chicago. Had he anything to do with the case?"

"I think so—yes. I have a letter that he received from Lockheim, written just before Lockheim died."

"I'd like to see it."

"You will. Let me put the whole package together first. It will make more sense then."

"You handle it your way, John."

Harbizon got up, spoke his thanks, and left before he had to say any more.

Because he hadn't given the matter any advance thought, Harbizon had expected Harold Horowitz to be some kind of a kid. Possibly the fact that Helen Chow referred to him as her boyfriend had influenced him, but he should have known that any young woman of her sophistication wouldn't have been tied up with a juvenile. As it was, Horowitz was close to forty and had the philosophy of a pile driver.

"I don't know why in hell you've come to see me," he said. "I don't know a damn thing about the death of San Marco. I told your partner, Dietrich, that when he came down here and took up more than an hour of my time."

His office was a small one, uncarpeted, and with no particular amenities. It didn't suggest that Harold Horowitz's time was as valuable as he himself seemed to think. He was officially a statistician, but that didn't appear to limit the scope of his activity.

"I'm sure you were willing to give an hour to help clear up a murder." Harbizon's tone was deceptively mild.

"Goddamn it, I'm getting sick of this! Just because I used to go with San Marco's mistress, now I'm being hounded by you city employees. You're exceeding your authority, mister. I don't like you, and I don't give a damn what you're trying to do. Is that clear enough?"

"It's clear to me that you're a complete horse's ass," Harbizon snapped back. "Any time reasonable questions are put to you by duly constituted authorities, you'd damn well better answer them. If you get handed a subpoena, you're required to answer it. It's part of the price you pay for the privilege of living in this country. And that's one of the most valuable things you'll ever have."

Horowitz sneered at him, and made sure that Harbizon saw the curl of his lips. "The only thing I give a damn about is money. Money means power, and that's the name of the game."

Harbizon had a reason for appearing to remain patient. "There are some things money won't buy."

"Horseshit. Fifty grand will get you a degree from any college in the country. An ambassadorship costs twice that." He waved a rejecting hand in front of Harbizon's face. "You haven't any, because you're only a cop. Already you're done for. Now how about getting out of my hair. The market's open and I'm not making a dime sitting here talking to you."

Harbizon timed it as he got up. He started to turn and then suddenly faced Horowitz again. "One question: Isn't it true that you had demolition training in the Army?"

"So what of it?" Horowitz snapped. "Can I help it if I was drafted?"

Cecil Forrester received Harbizon with the same

dignified and courteous manner that he had used at their first meeting. He showed his guest into his private office, picked up the phone, and instructed his secretary to hold all of his calls. That done, he settled back in his chair and offered his full attention. "How are you coming with your investigation?" he asked.

Harbizon maintained a completely relaxed attitude. "Quite well, all things considered. I came by to get the answers to a very few questions, if you don't mind. I've been spending most of the past three days gathering further background material on some of the people who figure in the case."

"Am I included?"

"Yes, Mr. Forrester, you are."

That caused the financial adviser to lean back in his chair and reflect for several seconds. When he finally spoke, he chose his words most carefully. "It was my belief that I was assisting you, in a small way, with some professional information about the stock market. I was not aware that I was a suspect."

Harbizon answered with equal care. "I didn't use that word, Mr. Forrester, nor do I intend to. But I would appreciate some answers, as I said."

"All right, go ahead."

"At my request, you made some inquiries concerning a possible next victim in this series of stock market murders. You mentioned that you were very discreet."

"I was."

"You did consult two other people."

"That's correct, but I put it on the basis that I wanted some information for purely personal reasons. You see, I too had a connection with Sphinx Wire and Cable, but in my case it was a disaster. I covered myself by asking if I might be a likely candidate to be eliminated."

That was an angle Harbizon had not considered. "You covered yourself very well indeed, I have to agree. In your opinion, Mr. Forrester, could either of the people you consulted unintentionally have mentioned your inquiry?"

"Absolutely not. One of them is the president of Sphinx, a man I have known intimately for many years and trust completely. The other is a financial adviser like myself whom I have also known for some time—well before I got into this business, as a matter of fact."

Harbizon appeared to be thinking carefully. Actually he was, planning just how he was going to put the next key question. "This is absolutely off the record, sir. It is my understanding that you were once in Intelligence work. Could this other gentleman possibly have a similar background?"

Forrester became extremely cautious. He waited some time and then spoke totally without visible emotion. "We were once associated for some time under conditions of great mutual trust. That's as far as I'm prepared to go. He did not, and will not talk, I'll guarantee it. You have my unreserved word that I did not. Even my secretary, who is totally trustworthy, doesn't know about those calls."

"Thank you very much."

"You're welcome, lieutenant. I'm sorry that everything I had to tell you was negative. I fear that I wasn't much help."

Harbizon stood up, calmly and easily. "On the contrary, sir, you've brought me quite a bit closer to my objective."

He fully expected after that to have Forrester ask him if he knew who had done the killings. When that obvious question didn't come, his opinion of the investment specialist rose proportionately. He left the office after making the usual polite statements, got back into his car, and headed up to see Dietrich.

In Los Angeles, Hatch and Marlow wrote up an interim final report on the murder of Ben Sorenson. It contained a good deal of data, particularly bearing on the private life of the dead broker, and included all of the definite evidence that the capable team had been able to gather. Every canyon resident had been seen and questioned, most of the people in Sorenson's office had been searchingly investigated, and all of them had been interviewed in depth. Several lady friends of the deceased, married and otherwise, were compelled to unburden themselves concerning their relations with the dead man. When it had all been summed up it gave a very clear picture of Ben Sorenson, the considerable swinger, the girl with whom he had been living at the time of his death, and the exact way in which the killing had been done.

But it did not contain the name of the man who had been under the house. It did contain the statement that until some new evidence or fresh data came to light, the investigation was suspended. A murder case is never closed until it is solved, but every available avenue had been exhausted, and it wasn't only a case of insufficient evidence—it was a case of no clues whatsoever as to the identity of the killer. As luck would have it, every one of the eleven clients of Ben Sorenson who had lost heavily on Sphinx Wire and Cable had been able to prove a clear and solid alibi for the time of the murder. Without exception they had been asleep in their homes and had other family members to back them up.

Marlow sent a copy of the report to Harbizon together with a covering letter. He asked to be posted immediately on any new developments.

In Chicago, Hanratty had also come to a dead end. The tenants of the high-rise apartment where Irving Brown had lived were notably uncooperative. They were paying premium rates for privacy, and they had no interest whatsoever in the dead man who had embarrassed them by splattering himself on the sidewalk in front of their exclusive building. The Brown apartment was sold within a week to a new tenant, or rather two: a pair of young men who were the owners of a highly successful small chain of beauty parlors. They charged astronomical prices and paid a good share of their earnings to a most efficient publicity agent. None of the other tenants took the least notice of them when they moved in.

Medical examination of the dead man had yielded very little. He had been drinking, but only moderately. Definitely he had not given himself one or two strong jolts before going over the railing. The amount of alcohol in his blood stream had been consistent with what he had drunk at his lady friend's apartment, according to her account. Brown's own apartment had yielded no clues other than the misplaced throw rug and the unmarred surface of the new paint on the terrace.

No one had been seen going either in or out of the rear service entrance, but it had been a foul night and, understandably, no one had been looking. Delivery vans were always coming at all hours—in particular, liquor store deliveries were often made well after midnight. Not a single witness could be found who would admit to having seen a stranger in the corridors, or anything unusual at all. Hanratty knew well that if any of the tenants *had* seen anything, they would never admit it to the police and thereby get involved. They all knew that it was a murder case, and they wanted no part of it.

Hanratty put it on the back burner. There were too many other things that cried for his attention.

Then the grinding work began. Harbizon patiently put in day after day, often until late at night, searching for fragments of evidence that might help him to make a case. Time after time he ran into a dead end, but when that happened he made a note or two and then started off on a new tack.

He made a trip to the Sphinx Wire and Cable Company and talked to several of the company officers, notably the comptroller. He was taken on an extensive tour of the plant facilities and formed his own estimate of the efficiency of the firm in producing its military hardware. He went to Washington and talked with some procurement specialists. From them he obtained records and a large amount of other data.

A broker in Boylesport supplied him with a price chart of the stock of Sphinx Wire and Cable. He spent more than a day correlating the purchase orders, the delivery dates, and the payment schedules with the fluctuations of the market price of the stock. He got a complete set of the publicity releases that the company had put out for the past year and studied those in reference to the stock price chart.

Lieutenant Walchewski of the NYPD helped him to obtain records on the transactions of Nathan Lockheim, Simon Korngold, and Ben Sorenson. It was less easy to trace the transactions of William San Marco because he had been the stock specialist and, therefore, every transaction, legitimate or otherwise, had passed through his hands. As he worked, he made it a business to read the *Wall Street Journal* every day. He was rewarded by a barrage of news concerning new regulatory bills in Congress, SEC actions, new trading restriction proposals, and other reforms that appeared to be coming from all directions.

From the New York Public Library he obtained a list of all of the available works dealing with explosive demolition and tried to track down who had drawn out those particular books during the past several months. That proved to be too mammoth a task, and he was forced to abandon it. Trying from the other direction, he found that the library was unable to tell him all of the books that a certain card holder had taken out. It was explained to him a number of times that the city was in acute financial straits and many normal services had been suspended.

It was slow, it was energy-sapping, but all of it had to be done. He did glean a few fragments here and there, all of a circumstantial nature. He felt consciously that he probably could have built some sort of a case against every person connected with the whole matter, but any real conclusive data, information that would tell him that he was at last on the right track, could not be found.

When he had done all that he could, and had put together as much as he had been able to glean from every source, he decided that it was time for him to fulfill an obligation. He had given his promise, and he was the kind of a man who considered that an unpaid obligation. He put in a call to the office of Burroughs and Schneider and asked when they could get together.

"Have you got something for us?" Schneider asked, quick interest in his voice.

"Possibly yes, but we will have to meet somewhere that's out of sight and where we won't be interrupted."

"Just tell me one thing," the columnist asked. "We're busy as hell right now. Will it be worth taking the time? No offense, but it's never been like this before."

"If I were you, I'd come," Harbizon said. "I have something to give you, and I warn you that I'm going to ask for something in return."

"Fair enough. Hang on."

The line was quiet for almost a half minute, then Schneider was back. "Is it hot?" he asked.

"It's hot."

"Then we can make it this afternoon, after three. Where?"

"On the parking lot of Palisades Park. Don't look for a police car."

"Hey, man, that's in Jersey."

"I know, but your faces are too well known in New York. Even though it's just across the river, Jersey is a different matter. Have you got wheels?"

"Oh sure, no sweat about that. OK, on the lot at four o'clock. How's that?"

"Fine. One thing—don't tell *anyone*, except your partner, that we're meeting."

"Depend on it. And you know that we'll protect a source if we have to go to jail for it."

"I appreciate that," Harbizon told him, "because some of this is police sensitive."

"Say no more. See you at four."

The line went dead.

Harbizon took his lunch in a bar that specialized
in much better than average food at a price that had
prevailed five years before. He had hoped to eat
quietly and in peace, but a television set that was on
kept intruding itself into his consciousness. He had
seldom seen television during the daytime, and the
barrage of commercials that bombarded him made
him gratefully aware of what he had been missing.
He tried to give his full attention to his food and to
the important matters he wanted to review in his
mind, but the ubiquitous TV continued to hammer
at him.

With a burst of electronic siren sounds the set
launched into the second half of a many times rerun
police drama. Actors in uniform, doing their best to
look like policemen, carried on their procedures as
the screenwriter had imagined them to be. In the
position of a captive audience Harbizon watched
and generously decided that the several absurdities
were not the actors' fault—they were only doing as
they were directed.

When the suspects appeared on screen, they were
prototypes for Professor Lombroso's concept of
criminal man. They snarled with well-schooled
technique, jumped into a car, and took off in a burst
of burning rubber.

An over-aggressive young pitchman appeared on
screen holding a product in his hand. He enthused
about it violently and for a triumphant conclusion a

beautiful woman rushed into the arms of the background man who had had the great wisdom to use the right mouthwash. It must have been potent stuff, Harbizon decided, for the girl to have detected its use from twenty feet away. The pitchman came back for a few seconds more, then there was a preposterous playlet in a laundry where the right soap was about to prove . . .

Harbizon made a determined effort to ignore the tube and return to his lunch. He would have walked out, but the food was good and he was still hungry. He ate and drank to wash it down, forcing the voice of the TV out of his mind. He did it so successfully he managed to ignore the next two commercials completely. Then the volume level dropped and the police drama was resumed.

The car chase was on. It was good visual stuff with the stunt drivers coaxing the maximum performance they could out of their specially equipped cars. At last the chief suspect was trapped on a bridge. He whipped out a gun and fired several shots at the police who were closing in on him. He hit no one, despite the fact that the usual precautions essential in such cases were not followed. Then the hero cop of the series raised his handgun and fired.

It was obvious that the suspect had been fatally hit. He teetered for a few seconds at the railing, then the camera shifted angle as the stunt man did a carefully managed fall into the river. The police turned away. No one seemed interested in recovering the body, and the available witnesses were ig-

nored. The tube cut to a model who danced in a thin
gown in the sunlight to show how beautifully her
hair had responded to the sponsor's shampoo.

Harbizon finished his meal, paid, and left.

As he drove in toward the city he reflected on the
police drama that he had just seen: so similar to
hundreds of others conjured up to formula to entertain an audience popularly supposed to be at a mental age of ten years.

The ending of his own case, when it eventually
came, would not be a spectacular chase ending in
bursts of gunfire. The great arrests of history had
often been made quietly. Some of the most desperate
criminals taken into custody had been asleep or had
yielded without a struggle. But that sort of thing did
not make TV fare.

However, that kind of thinking was getting him
nowhere. He had a job to do, and what was more, it
would have to be very carefully done. He was about
to skate on some very thin ice indeed, and he would
need to have all of his wits about him to pull it off.

He drove across New York with the feeling that
he knew the city intimately, but that the city would
never know him. New York as a city, he decided,
had one policy—it didn't give a damn. The George
Washington Bridge took him across the Hudson and
into New Jersey. As he drove nearer to the place
where he hoped to make a deal, he looked at the
parade of totally uninspired houses crowded together to provide for as many people as possible within a
minimum of space and wondered if the people who

lived in them were sentimental about their homes—
if to them one of the identical structures seemed any
different than the others.

"And this is the room where our Alice was
born . . ."

"I spent the better part of five months fixing up
these cabinets, but now it's like a new kitchen . . ."

"Dad—mother—this is Cecilie, the girl I've been
telling you about . . ."

". . . just two days after our fortieth anniversary.
He felt just fine when he went to bed. He drank his
coffee just like always, then about two in the morning . . ."

He jerked his mind away from that channel and
thought once again about the beautifully produced
annual report put out by Sphinx Wire and Cable.
The agency had done a fine job, and the messages to
the stockholders over the signatures of the principal
officers of the company told in just the right confident tones of the increased profits for the past year,
of the satisfactory disposal of a small division that
had not been returning a profit, and of the very
substantial backlog of confirmed government orders
that would keep the plant at close to capacity for the
next three and a half years.

He wondered, savagely, if many of the people
who lived in these uninspired, depressing homes had
read that glowing report, had put their faith in it,
and had invested their money in the company that
had to do well because of the government orders.
The United States Government would not go out of

business. It was the world's best and most reliable customer. And, according to the report, the quality of Sphinx products had never been higher, and the new line of shielded cables was a major advance produced by the research division.

He could well have put his money into Sphinx itself. And at the end of the report there had been the auditor's statement that the whole thing had been examined by them, and in their opinion, it was a true and accurate statement of the company's conditions as of the close of business on . . .

It *was* a good company, and he knew from his visit to the Pentagon that its products were first-rate. The stock should have held its value, it should have advanced, and the stockholders should have been rewarded for their confidence and trust. But then Nathan Lockheim had begun his manipulations, and suddenly SWC had begun a series of gyrations, aided and abetted by William San Marco, the man who found his own name inadequate for his daily use.

Lockheim had made money, great amounts of money to keep that obscene wife of his in French pastries and whipped cream. He had made the money, but by no standard that Harbizon knew had he *earned* it. He had taken it away from people who had never wanted to play his game in the first place—people whom the stock market called "investors."

Probably almost all of them had bought what they had thought of as "securities" and then had watched the papers, hoping for some gradual appreciation. They had ended up losing millions, and then Nathan Lockheim, in the words of his wife, had had his ass blown off. As far as Harbizon was concerned, he would be briefly mourned and little missed. His sole contribution to society had been to take other people's money away, and that was not much of an obituary.

It was ten minutes to four when Harbizon reached the amusement park, giving him a little time to put his mind in order and to make sure that he knew what he was going to do. Five minutes later another car arrived, circled, and then came up to where he was waiting. He saw at a glance that both Bert Schneider and Gene Burroughs had come, so they had taken him at his word when he had told them that he had something hot to give them.

Harbizon got out of his car and walked the short distance over to where the other vehicle had stopped. He bent over and spoke to Burroughs who was driving. "Have you got your car equipped with a tape recorder or anything like that?" he asked.

"Absolutely not," Burroughs said. "You have our word on it."

"Good. But somebody might still be interested in what we're doing here, and I don't want to have to identify myself. There's a coffee shop a short distance from here that has a large back room with private booths. At this hour it should be close to empty."

"You lead the way; we'll follow."

Harbizon got back into his car and drove to the coffee shop. His surmise had been accurate—the rear section was empty and closed. A word to the manager took care of that, and when he sat down with the columnists they were entirely by themselves.

A waitress came and took their order for coffee and some Danish rolls. That was enough to guarantee their being left alone for a few minutes. When the food had been served, and the waitress had left, the two columnists looked at Harbizon, waiting for him to speak.

"In the first place," he began, "we are now in the state of New Jersey which relieves me of certain restraints. I'm a peace officer in the state of New York, but my authority doesn't extend across the Hudson."

"Understood," Schneider said.

"Now, this whole business of stock market killings has been quite a bit different from the usual murder investigation. There is no legal excuse for taking human life promiscuously, and it can't be condoned no matter how much some particular individual offends society or outrages the people around him. If he commits a capital offense and is convicted of it, then society will dispose of him. If he is in a position where the law doesn't reach him, then the proper remedy is to change the law."

He stopped, but neither of his listeners interrupted the silence. He had put himself on record and they understood that.

"Now we come to some specifics," Harbizon went on. "I'm going to keep my promise to you and give you certain facts. Under no circumstances are you to refer to me as the source."

Both of the columnists spoke at once, but it was Schneider who came out on top. "No court in the land can make us talk," he said. "And that issue is pretty well settled by now. If we ever did start talking, that would be the day that we would be out of business."

"Then we understand each other. Now here are the facts I promised to you. You can publish them if you want to, and I don't have to caution you to watch the laws of libel. You may be walking pretty close to the edge."

Burroughs responded to that. "You can bet your last dollar, lieutenant, that we won't overstep the line. That's the first thing every newspaperman learns—what he can legally say and what he can't. We check each other on that constantly."

Harbizon broke off a piece of roll and took his time eating it. He was in no hurry, and he wanted to keep the pace of the conversation as he had planned it. He drank a little coffee and then began once more. "There was a man in Chicago named Irving W. Brown. He ran a market tip sheet and did a good deal of business on the side as a trader himself. He was splitting commissions with a brokerage house in Chicago, but that's incidental. He was heavily involved in Sphinx Wire and Cable. He knew Nathan Lockheim, and I have a letter that Lockheim wrote to him shortly before Lockheim died. That last is off the record; you know nothing of any such letter."

"Agreed," Schneider said.

"Now, the evidence of the letter, plus a very careful check of what happened to the Sphinx stock shortly thereafter, indicates that Lockheim had promised some sort of deal to Brown. At least Brown's tip sheet played right into Lockheim's hands."

"I don't see why Brown would do that," Burroughs interrupted. "If he deliberately printed the wrong information in his tip sheet, then he would lose subscribers and his reputation would be damaged."

"Exactly the way I see it," Harbizon agreed. "I think, therefore, that Lockheim crossed him up. Brown was smart enough to catch it in time and save his own bacon, but the letter was out and he couldn't recall it."

Schneider whistled softly. "You've been doing your homework," he said, "and it is one hell of a story."

"I think there's more," Burroughs said. "Please go on, lieutenant."

"Some more facts, and I emphasize that they are facts not necessarily related. It is next to impossible to establish the time when a bomb is rigged or planted, because if it is successful, all of the pertinent evidence is destroyed. In the case of Lockheim's car, I do know that the bomb was wired to it sometime after he parked it at the station, but I haven't been able to narrow it from there. No one saw anything, and I can't come up with any evidence to the contrary."

"Leaving an open period of eight hours or more," Burroughs declared.

"True. Now, gentlemen, I have been able to establish one thing. Brown lived alone and didn't report his movements to anyone. But according to his mistress, on the day that Lockheim went up in front of his estate, Brown was out of town. She thinks he was in New York. What's more, he had said something to her about seeing a man who had crossed him up badly."

"Eureka!" Schneider said, keeping his voice down.

"How about the time when dear Mr. San Marco got his?" Burroughs asked.

"Brown was still out of town," Harbizon said, "but he was often out of town, gathering information for his tip sheet—or so he said. In the absence of his own testimony, and that isn't available, Brown has no alibi for the time of either of the murders. He was in Chicago when Simon Korngold was run down, but that has been put down as an accident and therefore the timing isn't important."

"There was another killing in California," Burroughs said. He ventured that cautiously, leaving it to Harbizon whether he wanted to talk about it or not.

"As far as I can trace, Brown was in Chicago when that happened. However, the man who was

killed, Ben Sorenson, was screwing every female he
could find, married or otherwise. He also was a
market operator and cost a lot of people some huge
sums, enough to make him some very strong
enemies."

"You're suggesting, then, that his death was not
directly related to the Lockheim and San Marco
killings?"

"I could make a good case for that theory."

Schneider was thinking intently. "If what you say
is true, and the Sorenson death was a separate thing,
then that could revive the Jewish angle. I hope to
God that I'm wrong, but it could be a combination—
a campaign against men who were stock market manipulators *and* Jewish . . ."

"You can drop it," Harbizon said. "I don't believe
that there is a Jewish angle, and I'm as grateful as
you are. Brown, incidentally, was also Jewish, so I
checked exhaustively on all known bigoted organizations and violent individuals. I'll stake my reputation that religion had nothing to do with these
murders."

"We'll buy that," Burroughs said. "Please go
on."

Harbizon did. "Now let me give you a possible
reconstruction. Irving Brown got a letter from Lockheim laying out a plan. Brown went along and published in his tip sheet exactly what Lockheim had
asked for. Brown took a position himself in the
Sphinx Wire and Cable stock, and all looked well.
Then, according to the phone company, Lockheim

called Brown in Chicago."

"When?" Burroughs asked quickly.

"Two days before he died. Thereupon, Brown left town, presumably for New York."

"Is there any evidence that Brown knew anything about explosives?" Schneider asked.

"He was never in any branch of the service; he managed to duck it, and I didn't find any other lead in that direction."

"But he could have been briefed, or he could have hired someone."

"The briefing is possible, but I can't see him finding a man to do that job for him. Too risky. Now here's some more. I dug up Brown's name, never mind how, and went to see him. I called him from the airport and asked for an immediate appointment. He refused until I told him that I was a police officer and that his life might be in danger. At that time I specifically told him that I was from the Boylesport Police. He didn't ask me why anyone from that jurisdiction wanted to see him; he didn't even ask where Boylesport was."

"He could have known that Lockheim lived there," Schneider interjected.

"That's true, of course. Now Brown told me that he would be out earlier in the evening, but to come to his apartment house and to wait in the lobby. When I got there, a little early, Brown was dead, lying on the pavement where he could well have hit had he jumped from his own terrace. Those are the facts that I promised to give to you."

The waitress came and warmed their coffee cups. Harbizon smiled his thanks and then let the reporters consider the information he had just given them.

"It all makes very good sense," Burroughs said at last. "Brown was double-crossed by Lockheim, and his whole position was undermined. He went to New York. Lockheim was killed and so was San Marco, who we know was involved with him in the stock manipulation. Brown returned to Chicago. After a while a lieutenant of the Boylesport Police is suddenly in town and wants to see him that same night. Personally, I would have run for it, but Brown went the other route."

"And you can't arrest a dead man," Schneider said.

"No, I can't."

"Now, can we print the facts that you just gave us, except the part about the letter?"

"Yes."

"I take it that we have this exclusively," Burroughs said.

"That's right—you do."

"Lieutenant, I don't know how we can thank you enough."

"Never mind that. Do you agree that I've lived up to my part of our bargain?"

Both columnists spoke at the same time, then Schneider stopped and let Burroughs go ahead. "Absolutely. But before we print, we've got to get some more background on Brown. We don't know what kind of a man he was."

"Not a lot different from Lockheim and San Marco," Harbizon supplied. "I ran quite a careful check on him. He was a heavy trader and used his own tip sheet to increase the odds in his favor. He had a reputation for ruthlessness."

"Did he play around with a lot of women?"

"No, not according to the picture that I got. He had a steady woman, and that seemed to satisfy him."

"Then why didn't he marry her?"

"He couldn't."

"Oh!"

"Her husband's in service overseas. Sit on that."

There was another silence. When it had run its course, Harbizon broke it with a question. "Would you care for a little more?"

"Hell, yes," Burroughs answered.

"Then I'd better begin by telling you something further about police work. A crime is committed, and we are called in. From that moment on we have, substantially, two jobs. We have to find out who is responsible for the crime and determine the motive. Then, after that, we have to get enough hard evidence, by strictly legal means, to establish proof in court of his guilt. We have to give the district attorney a case solid enough that he knows he has a good chance of securing a conviction despite anything that the defense may try, and you can take it from me that they will try anything."

"I think we both understand that," Burroughs said.

"I hadn't quite made my point," Harbizon came back. "Because of certain legal rules, and some court decisions that have been handed down in the past, we often find ourselves in the position of knowing who committed a certain crime, but for one reason or another we can't make a case strong enough for the DA to take into court."

Schneider wasn't paying full attention. "There's something I can't figure out," he said. "How did Brown ever manage to put that bomb on Lockheim's car without somebody seeing him?"

"I think I can answer that," Harbizon replied. "It goes back to Mr. Chesterton and his invisible man. What is the most common thing you could see anyone doing to a car, by way of repair that is?"

"Changing a tire," Burroughs responded.

"Exactly. No one would notice or pay any attention to someone changing a tire. This is pure speculation, but I can see a service truck or van, or even a private car, pulling onto the lot and then going about changing a tire on Lockheim's car. The risk factor would be relatively small, because no one would notice Lockheim's tires unless one happened to be conspicuously flat. The repair truck drives on the lot, out comes the jack, and the wheel is lifted off the ground. From that point on it looks perfectly all right, because a flat tire, once it is jacked up, almost always resumes its normal shape."

"He would need a key," Schneider said.

"Yes, or a small tool that would pop open the trunk for him. Remember, he knew that the car was going to be wrecked, so a few extra scratches wouldn't cause him any great concern."

"And under the guise of changing a tire, he could attach the bomb."

"Something like that. An ordinary tire change wouldn't even be noticed, or if it happened to be seen, it would be forgotten almost at once. We don't remember things unless we take some note of them first."

"And if the car was parked some distance down the line on the lot, no one would be able to recognize Brown later anyway," Burroughs contributed.

"Quite right, any more than he would be able to recognize you. Now let me back up for a moment. I thought at first that these killings were someone's revenge for having lost heavily on Sphinx Wire and Cable. Later I discarded that theory, and I saw that particular company more as a thread that leads all through the case. It is a definite connecting link, but the death of the broker, Ben Sorenson, on the Coast should have narrowed the possible suspects down to his own clients."

"I thought you said that the incident in California wasn't part of the picture," Schneider cut in.

"No, I didn't say that. I said that I could make a good case for that theory, but I didn't say that I bought it. As a matter of fact, I believe that it was very much a part of the whole picture."

Both columnists remained silent, even though Harbizon gave them plenty of time to comment if they wanted to.

"Now there are certain pieces of information that I collected which fit together in quite another way," Harbizon continued. "First of all, it was clear from the first that whoever was behind these deaths had a much-better-than-average knowledge of the stock market. The point was made to me that a person could find out who a floor specialist in a certain stock was, but that it was almost literally never done. A cheated or disappointed investor would blame his stockbroker first of all, then perhaps his brokerage company, and possibly a publicized speculator. You remember the Insull case and more recently Cornfeld. These men were well covered by the press, and their manipulations were exposed over a wide area. But Lockheim had never had any such publicity, and San Marco was virtually unknown except on the trading floor of the exchange. So it is an obvious conclusion that it was not merely a furious investor who had lost because of these men's activities that was responsible. It had to be someone who had a much greater knowledge of the whole stock market setup."

He stopped and drank a little coffee, waiting for any questions. Both reporters were listening to him intently now, which was the way he wanted it.

"Now the Lockheim killing was very neatly done by someone who knew his business, but it is surprising how much information you can get on almost any subject if you take the trouble to really look it up. You know that, of course, being reporters. The San Marco killing had something about it that disturbed me, and that was the manner in which he was shot. The man who killed him carefully used an undersized bullet trick that is very cute indeed, but there was no need for it. Ever since Saturday night specials became a drug on the market, almost anyone can get one, use it once, and then throw it away. So I asked myself, why would anyone go to the trouble of working that particular trick unnecessarily. The only reason would be to prevent the identification of a known gun, or one that the police could obtain if necessary. But no such gun has appeared anywhere along the line. For example, neither of you has a licensed firearm. I looked it up."

"What's your conclusion, then?" Burroughs asked.

"I think it was done to confuse the issue, or else to display virtuosity for its own sake. You see, it's an interesting aspect of these killings that the MO's differed so radically. One man was blown up, a second was shot, a third was electrocuted, and a fourth was pushed over a railing. In all four cases some refined technique was used, possibly to suggest that some undercover agents, friendly or otherwise, were at work. Or else someone who had had that kind of training."

"Most interesting," Schneider said.

"Now I also noticed another fact," Harbizon went on. "At one stage of the game I wanted to contact someone for some detailed information about the stock market, and I consulted you. You will remember that, I'm sure. You were kind

enough to give me the name of Cecil Forrester, and
then, in the next breath, you supplied the rather
unusual information that he had an Intelligence
background—that he had been, in your words, 'a
James Bond type.'

"For men trained to keep your mouths shut about
confidential information, that was an astounding
thing for you to tell me. Later, when I saw Mr.
Forrester, I brought the subject of his Intelligence
activity up twice, and both times he very carefully
avoided making any statement, even though I had
assured him that our conversation was totally confidential. You can see the obvious conclusion that I
drew. I didn't think that you were trying to impli-
cate him, because he's a man who keeps a careful
schedule, and he was able to prove an alibi when I
asked him for one. But there was a certain odor
about it—one that is commonly known as 'red
herring.'

"Now, gentlemen, a most interesting little point.
I've already established the fact that Sphinx Wire
and Cable was a thread, carefully maintained, that
runs through this whole case. With that in mind you
will remember that I asked you if there were any
more like Lockheim, San Marco, and Korngold, and
you gave me a generalized answer that there were
probably some on the floor of the exchange and possibly a few more scattered around the country. I
noted at the time that although the Korngold killing
was accidental, you had built up a thick file on
him—you told me so in so many words. In view of

later events, I wonder how you ever overlooked telling me about Brown in Chicago. Especially since he published a nationally distributed tip sheet that you couldn't possibly have missed. And, as I just told you, it ran recent material on Sphinx Wire and Cable to please Nathan Lockheim. You do know that tip sheet, don't you?"

"Yes," Burroughs answered.

"I might add, if you're still interested, that I managed to obtain three other opinions on who might possibly be the next victim. All three of my consultants came up with several names, but Brown was the only one who was mentioned by all three. *They* certainly knew of him. And he was a prize bet because no other name was duplicated even once. Subsequent events would seem to prove that my information was correct. Brown was indeed the most likely next victim."

"I thought he was a suicide," Schneider said.

"Come now," Harbizon answered. "I just told you a few minutes ago that he was pushed. If you wanted to question the point, that would have been the time. No, gentlemen, he was pushed, and something about his body lying on the sidewalk gave me a very important lead. I already suspected that he wasn't a suicide. And then I saw evidence of that in his apartment."

"Naturally, we're most interested in what you're saying," Burroughs declared.

"I thought you might be. When I was in Chicago I had the feeling that I was missing something, but I couldn't bring it into focus. Later it came to me. As I saw Brown's body, even though it was badly squashed, I noticed that he had been a big burly man. He had been in the prime of life, so he was obviously of much more than average strength and vigor. He definitely didn't want to die.

"He died when he was somehow compelled to stand on a small rug on the terrace of his apartment, and then he was levered over. I was supposed to come to that conclusion because the rug had not been replaced where it belonged, and that would only have taken a few seconds. So I began to reconstruct. Certainly he didn't go out on the terrace willingly—it was a wretched, wet night. I worked out several possible ways that it might have been done, but the interesting feature was that in every case two people were required. Would you like to hear the theory I like best?"

"Please," Schneider said.

"Very well. I see two men coming into the apartment house through the rear entrance. Presumably they were making a delivery, and I've already established that although the front door is constantly watched to keep out unwanted visitors, the service entrance is often left uncovered at night—a bad breach of security. Nobody saw them, which was their good fortune, but few people were going in or out that night. They got into Brown's apartment, and I admit I don't know if they picked the lock or had gotten hold of a key. Then they checked through the apartment, found the throw rug, and made very good use of it. From that apartment they could see people arriving or leaving the building; you remember that Brown's body was just a few feet from the front entrance. When they saw Brown arrive, they went into their act.

"When Brown came in, he found what he believed to be burglars ransacking his apartment. One of them put a gun on him, took his wallet, and ordered him to go onto the terrace. As a wild guess, I would cover a small bet that it was the same gun that sent San Marco to join his ancestors. Anyhow, with a gun held on him, Brown was forced to obey. When he had been seen coming, the rug had been put on the terrace. Then the other supposed burglar came, said something like 'Let's get out of here,' and then yanked the rug when Brown wasn't expecting it. I don't say that it happened that way—that's only one possibility—but I am confident that no one person could have overpowered Brown or forced him to jump from his own balcony. He would have to be tricked since it is obvious that he wouldn't willingly kill himself against the threat of a gun. A man of his build would have rushed the gunman and taken his chances of only being wounded. Also, his temperament was not meek and submissive. A single attacker would have had his hands very full with Mr. Irving Brown.

"So that is what put me on the track of a possible collaboration. The only other alternative was a gang type of thing, and that didn't fit the evidence at all. Now you can begin to see the picture emerging—a job that obviously required two people, persons well acquainted with the stock market and its many aspects, and what's more, persons with a very close mutual understanding. It did come to me that whenever we've talked together, neither one of you has ever said 'I'—on every occasion, including today, it has always been 'we.' "

"In all candor, wouldn't you agree that what you're suggesting is a bit farfetched?" Schneider asked.

"I don't know," Harbizon answered. "You see there's one other thing that was quite significant. The death of Brown was mentioned in the papers, particularly in the *Wall Street Journal*. No weather report was attached to the story. But when I talked to you gentlemen about it, you brought up the point that it had been a particularly foul and rainy night in Chicago, a rather clear indication to me that you had been there. Weather is never mentioned in a newspaper account of that kind unless it was a contributing factor, such as reporting that a plane crash took place during heavy rain and dense fog."

Harbizon drank the last of his coffee in an almost casual manner. "By the way, two other small points," he added. "You made the mistake of giving me a description of the building in which Brown lived. You wouldn't have known that unless you had called on him at some time, and if you had, you would have mentioned it before now. We must have missed each other by a fairly small margin. And perhaps you remember that once when I came to see you both, Bert was reported as being "out of town," and I talked to you, Gene, instead. That was the time that you gave me Forrester's name. And, interestingly enough, while Bert was gone, Ben Sorenson died in Los Angeles. That was a one-man job, and I must say, it was very expertly done."

Speaking very carefully, Gene Burroughs took up the conversation. "While we've been here," he said, "you made out quite a good case against Brown as the man behind these untimely deaths. Then you turned around and theorized about us. As a starter, you can't possibly have it both ways."

"Of course not," Harbizon agreed. "I gave you some information about Brown, and I'm afraid that I did present it in a way that could be construed as implicating him. The man is dead, he left no family, and there is no one to suffer in the possible event that he is eventually thought to be the stock market killer. You see, as I told you, no case can be advanced against a suspect unless there is enough hard evidence, or some reliable witnesses, or both, to support a prosecution."

Schneider cut in. "There's a point you mentioned before, when you were telling us about police work. You said specifically that your first job in any investigation was to find out who had done a certain thing, and establish the reason—determine the motive in other words. What motive would you ascribe to us, for instance?"

Harbizon retained his very casual manner. "I do have in mind a conversation we had together when you told me that the stock market killings had done wonders for your circulation and readership. As I recall, you said that these developments had made you almost as well known as Woodward and Bernstein. Some people could call that an extremely strong motive. Being right on top of a continuing major story, like the Watergate scandal that brought down the Nixon administration, could make a lifelong major reputation.

"Then there is another angle, one to which I have given a lot of thought. I told you that murder cannot be condoned, no matter who the victim is, and that is the law's position—and mine. In the case of the stock market killings, the victims were all exploiters of the public, human sharks who took advantage of our financial system to commit something close to legal robbery. Their elimination was a selective process, it is obvious, a kind of vigilantism that might have a small measure of justification in some people's eyes. You remember the old 'unwritten law' that we still hear about from time to time. These killings had even less justification, but the victims themselves are not too likely to be missed—I noted that. Only Lockheim was married and that, I was told, was strictly a business arrangement. I interviewed Mrs. Lockheim twice, once right after her husband had been killed, and she showed no signs of grief at all."

"So what happens now?" Schneider asked.

Harbizon became a bit more brisk. "Oh, that is all laid out. As I told you before, when we don't have enough evidence to make an arrest of a known guilty party, we lie in wait more or less for him to make his next move. Almost invariably we get him then. We're forewarned, we know who we're after, and under those circumstances we can gather damning evidence without any waste of time. In my previous job, before I came to Boylesport, we had a known hit man who had committed three brutal murders. When we had him pinpointed we kept a careful watch. On his fourth try we nailed him and, incidentally, saved the victim. And we had more than enough evidence for a conviction."

"Did you get it?" Burroughs asked.

"He copped out. There was no trial."

Bert Schneider looked at his partner and then went through the motions of stretching his legs under the table. "I don't know," he said. "It's just a feeling I have, but with all of the reform action that's going on now, the major clean-up that's been fifty years overdue, the new regulatory bills in Congress, and the sudden show of guts on the part of some governmental agencies, I don't believe that there are going to be any more violent deaths. What do you think, Gene?"

"I'm inclined to agree," Burroughs answered. "If, for instance, the major reform now going on had been the real objective, certainly it's already been achieved. From now on the public is going to be protected, and the Lockheims won't be able to exist anymore."

"There's a basic lesson behind all this," Harbizon

said. "Someday when you have a good opportunity, you might put this in your column. Every now and then some citizens become upset, angry, and even violent, but there is a remedy available to them. If certain judges consistently let off obviously guilty defendants on one pretext or another, they can be voted out of office. The same goes for politicians who put through legislation drastically reducing penalties for major crimes. You have the power of the press behind you. Use it to expose the people in office who deserve to be defeated or recalled. You can do that for the rest of your lives and stay completely within the law. They give Pulitzer Prizes for things like that."

"It's a good thought," Schneider agreed.

"You mentioned Woodward and Bernstein. You know what they did, and everything after that went strictly according to the Constitutional process. Ford became President, a new vice-president was named, and there was no violence whatever. As I see it, that's the way to do things. The means are there, and with your column, you can, as they say, move mountains. I hope that you will."

Burroughs signaled to the waitress. "This little refreshment is on us," he announced. "I hope we'll meet again soon."

"I hope so too," Harbizon answered. "Unofficially."

He left them and went outside by himself. Without looking back he got into his car and headed toward the George Washington Bridge. When he was once more on Manhattan Island, he pulled up at a convenient corner and made use of a phone booth.

Helen Chow answered on the third ring. When he heard her voice on the line it gave him a little stab of satisfaction. "This is John Harbizon," he said.

"Hello, John."

"I've been working on the Lockheim case, and now, I believe, I've got it wrapped up. That goes for the death of your late friend, San Marco, also."

"I'm so glad to hear that!" There was real warmth in her voice.

"We had talked once about getting together after the case was over. I wondered if by any chance . . ."

"As it happens I am—free that is. Where are you?"

"Upper Manhattan."

"Then why don't you come down and we'll have a drink together."

"And then I'd like to take you out to dinner."

"All right."

After she had hung up Harbizon pressed his lips together with satisfaction. She had had the very good sense not to ask him any questions over the telephone. If his luck held out, she might be intelligent enough not to ask him anything at all, knowing that if he wanted to tell her, he would.

As he started up his car once more, a major weight that he had been living with for some time had been lifted away. Also, he had the prospect of a most pleasant evening before him. He would never have met her if it had not been for the series of events that had begun in Boylesport.

He realized then that whatever Helen Chow had done in the past didn't mean a damn to him. She was more woman than he had ever known before, and he was more than willing to settle for that.

At that moment he knew that a policeman's lot could also be a happy one.